SUMMER

WILL

END

Also by Dorian Yeager

Cancellation by Death
Eviction by Death
Ovation by Death
Murder Will Out

SUMMER

WILL

END

Dorian Yeager

An Elizabeth Will/Dovekey Beach Mystery

St. Martin's Press

New York

Library of Congress Cataloging-in-Publication Data

Yeager, Dorian.
    Summer will end / by Dorian Yeager.—1st ed.
      p.   cm.
    ISBN 0-312-14743-0
    I. Title.
    PS3575.E363S8   1996
    813'.54—dc20   96-22111
                                 CIP

First Edition: December 1996

10 9 8 7 6 5 4 3 2 1

This book is dedicated to

Dr. Albert Franklin Yeager
Arlene Stepanek Yeager
Florence Will Yeager
and all the big and little Yeagers.

ACKNOWLEDGMENTS

Charles Donigian
and Columbia's Old Blue Rugby Football Club,
who know when to tour out of town;

Miss Elle's Verbal Sparring Team,
which knows better than to call in the morning;

and Jeremy and Gen,
who give me a reason to answer the phone at all.

SUMMER

WILL

END

PROLOGUE

MOONLIGHT SLICED THROUGH the venetian blinds and cut sharp ribbons across the face of the old man sprawled on the bed. The ivory chenille bedspread barely humped over the frail form.

Gashes of light flicked and tickled at the man's bony wrists and hands; the fog jigged a danse macabre beyond the cheap metal door that faced the deserted beach as the new electronic foghorn in the White Island lighthouse groaned.

As did the man.

His thrashing in the coarse muslin sheets crescendoed in a strangely beautiful ballet of its own: melodic, delicate in its rhythm, in an insidious counterpoint to the sweep of the lighthouse lantern.

White Island moaned emphatic punctuation to the tightening of the man's esophagus around the bile hurling upward from his stomach. Fragile fists contracted and relaxed. Crepy skin hanging from the man's neck relaxed as the remains of a sumptuous fried-clam dinner settled back into his stomach.

His labored gasping was swallowed by the lighthouse's electronic bleat and carried out to sea as though on the wings of an angel gull.

Vomit, squeezed up by the spasm of his diaphragm, was sucked heartily into his lungs, and rheumy powder-blue eyes sprang open as his heart labored for oxygen.

The man drowned in the remnants of his last ocean-fresh seafood platter at the precise moment that his wife of forty-nine years merrily called out "Bingo!" three blocks down the beach road.

ONE

Elizabeth Will was gratified to see the Dovekey Beach town common swarming with activity as she set up her stall of watercolor paintings.

The weather looked decent, and the town had sprayed to exterminate the mosquitoes during the dawn hours, so Elizabeth calculated that it would be a good forty-five minutes before she would have to slather on the insect repellant which always gave her such a suspicious rash. It was important to her that she look good for the day, and it had nothing to do with business.

Her father, Frank, had often advised her that the blemishes did nothing to encourage serious art buying.

"Unaesthetic, yah know," he offered that morning, in place of parental concern.

She advised him in return that he was not doing all that much to promote her career either, and that, perhaps, he ought to find another blood relative to harass for the duration of the festival.

Since he had immediately vacated the spot over her shoulder where he had been hovering, she assumed innocently that he had been listening to her.

Some people never learn. Or so they say in Dovekey Beach, New Hampshire—a place where talking overmuch is not highly regarded.

The Fourth of July fireworks had been a huge success the night before and camaraderie was running rampant this morning. For the first time in the small town's collective memory, Rollie Ouimet had managed to set every pyrotechnic charge without igniting himself or his jane-of-all-trades wife, Terri. This was not necessarily a relief to all. Terri's bullying of her husband had begun to get on people's nerves. In fine New England fashion, everyone agreed it was none of their business, *but* everyone also agreed that it was just a matter of time before Terri's meddling got her blown to hell. (And, unspoken, the belief that hell would just blow her right back, so what would be the point of all that trouble?) So, once a year the township held its breath waiting for what seemed the final and inevitable Independence from Terri Ouimet Day.

Still, this was the first year that, through "helping," Terri had not vitally singed her nearest-and-dearest long-suffering Rollie. Town chatter was that things might be looking up, though no one really believed it.

The adjoining town of Pebble Beach had scheduled its own festival for the same day.

The mayor of the much-maligned competition, Dick Dawley, swore on a stack of four-color tourism brochures that it was just coincidence, and everyone, in the best New England tradition, pretended to believe him. Even churlish Frank Will, who benevolently promised that Dick would be the honored guest at the next Masonic Temple's Robbie Burns extravaganza and, therefore, the recipient of the homemade haggis.

"To show our support," Frank claimed, "the least we can

do is gather together as one and watch Dick scarf down an oatmeal-stuffed sheep's gut."

Much to the amusement of her neighbors, Elizabeth ignored her father, who knew she never really ignored anything.

And people think Yankees are a cold, heartless breed.

Elizabeth snapped her longish strawberry blond hair into a rubber band to get it out of her face, and set a v-shaped bin into a hand-fashioned wooden cradle built to exhibit her less expensive, matted watercolor paintings. At her father's mercenary suggestion and out of economic desperation, there were more than the usual number of ultrapopular seascapes. Yes, even the ubiquitous rendering of Nubble Light.

She muttered as she worked, something she did more and more the longer she lived with her dad. It caused no concern anymore in a town so small that everyone knew the precise size and location of everyone else's birthmarks.

The pricier, framed paintings were already hung on the three-sided pegboard display behind Elizabeth. After hauling lobster traps with Frank at the crack of dawn, she had cannibalized her own art gallery to come up with enough items to make a decent showing at the festival sale.

Elizabeth checked her watch for the time and sped up her organizing. She had made a list that morning to include some spiffing up for herself. The last thing she wanted was to appear old and worn out.

If she had not been working both the fishing industry and the gallery, she would have had the leisure to realize how tired she looked. But the infamous Will family luck was on her side; there would be no self-indulgent minutes for quite a while.

For the locals, summer was a mess. The season was short, and for the last three years, the tourist dollars had been scarcer than hair on a halibut.

"No thanks to 'The Dick,' " Elizabeth groused to herself.

That would be her childhood companion, Dick Dawley—now mayor of the neighboring village of Pebble Beach.

Under Dawley's leadership, Pebble Beach had become a mecca for the generosity-challenged of the Northeast. He had slammed through zoning for seasonal trailer parks (so decorative) and cheapo motels. Beachfront properties were thrown up hastily, one atop another like a condominium of cards.

"One good hurricane and *whoosh!*" Elizabeth grunted and pounded a stake at the north end of her display.

Nonetheless, unlike Dovekey, Pebble Beach had lowered its property taxes two years in a row.

"Bastards!" Elizabeth grumbled under her breath and tied a bouquet of helium balloons to the wooden stake. To the confusion of the rest of the festival, "WELCOME HOME" was written in bright colors on each Mylar sphere. Elizabeth had tied and curled the long ribbons that held them herself. She had been looking forward to this day for months. There was nothing like a good reunion to warm a cooling spirit, she thought. Briefly.

"Biz!" Dick Dawley smacked Elizabeth on the back. "Damned if you don't look better every year!"

Elizabeth unconsciously scrolled her litany of complaints against her luck and her life before straightening up. She had managed to avoid Dawley for almost a year. Her time was up.

The mayor was tall and undernourished–looking, except for the ripple of middle-age bulge stretching at his pink polo shirt. Emblazoned on the left breast was the Pebble Beach logo: "Life's never rocky at Pebble Beach!!"

Yeah, Elizabeth commented to herself, then why is it named *Pebble* Beach: designer sand stippling? Despite the set of her jaw and stiffness of her full upper lip, still she was startled by Dick's swift smack on the back of her neck.

"Mosquito," he explained and grinned hugely in her direction, his eyes taking in the activity on the common. "You folks

6

over here in the cheap seats ought to use that new insecticide spray we're using next door." He spread his hand to display the splattered mosquito body and a small spray of blood. "Environmentally responsible, ya' know."

Elizabeth took Dick's wrist and pulled him toward her. His grin nearly burst his ruddy cheeks. He allowed himself to be directed. Just like prom night, Elizabeth thought with a shiver of self-loathing, only in reverse: pulling this time instead of slapping away.

Maybe I should move to the Czech Republic and start over. How hard could it be to learn a Slavic language? Well, she reasoned, *if I can't learn the language, I'll just tell everyone I'm an orphaned Canadian or something. No one will ever find me. I'll reinvent my past and never have to stick my arm up to the pit in bait ever again—literally or figuratively. I'll think of something before next season.*

Elizabeth smiled back coyly at The Dick and rubbed his palm across the thigh of his powder blue Bermuda shorts. The blood smeared downward from the brown splotch of crushed bug.

"Just swatting the little shits works, too," she deadpanned and turned back to her arranging. Elizabeth shook her head, her mouth crooked up at one side from compression, showing a small dimple.

"Speaking of little shits," Elizabeth heard her father offer from over her shoulder, "get out of the way, Dawley."

"Good to see you, Mr. Will," Dick answered, sounding for all the world exactly as he did on prom night. Well, maybe a little smarmier.

"I'll bet." Frank shouldered his way into the four-foot-square enclosure and set up a card table at the opening. Dawley inched himself carefully out onto the grassy area. Frank set up a hand-lettered sandwich board on the table reading "Good Art Cheap," which Elizabeth removed without a moment's hesitation. The Czech Republic was sounding better and better to her—except that, if she remembered correctly from the last post-card she had received, her runaway romance-novelist mother was currently attending a conference there. Elizabeth often had the sneaking suspicion that orphans had all the luck.

Frank shrugged amenably at the rejection of his marketing tool and ripped open a cardboard box measuring about a cubic yard.

Elizabeth opened a folding chair, placed the cheap-art sign on the seat—facedown—and sat. "Don't even think about it," she said, cuddling warm thoughts of Daddy Warbucks and, even, evil orphanage manager Miss Hannigan.

"Had them made up special," her father answered, ignoring her as always.

"I thought you were going to sell lobster stew with the volunteer fire department." She watched Frank unload stack upon stack of 3″ × 12″ papers. Of course, there probably isn't much lobster stew available in Prague, she thought, then added, "No, father, I am not going to baby-sit your libertarian propaganda this afternoon."

"Didn't ask you to," he said and moved her over to the side of the already-cramped space.

She was going to end up killing him. She knew it. She would finally go over the edge, bludgeon him to death with an ornately framed seascape, and spend the rest of her life in a high-security woman's prison.

Elizabeth realized she could live with that.

"God, Mr. Will!" Dick Dawley exclaimed in horror, which brought Elizabeth back from her fantasy. She looked at the Day-Glo orange bumper sticker Frank had adhered to the top of the card table.

It read: "If it's tourist season, why can't I shoot one?" Price: five dollars, no tax. Elizabeth wanted a cigarette very badly. If she remembered correctly, *everyone* smoked in the Czech Republic.

As luck would have it, her old buddy Ginny Philbrick was cutting through the growing crowd toward the Wills. Ginny's Chief of Police shield glistened in the summer sun, her uniform shirt was opened at the top two buttons, and a pack of cigarettes bulged at the pocket.

"Ginny, give me a cig," Elizabeth stuck out her hand. Ginny gave her the butt she was smoking.

"You quit," Ginny reminded her for friendship's sake. In fact, she didn't give a rat's ass. Then assessing the displayed bumper stickers, Frank, and Dick Dawley, Ginny tossed her Camels onto the card table.

"Heard about your trouble this mornin' " Dick gloated.

"What trouble?" Elizabeth lit a fresh cigarette from the stub she was holding. Frank arranged his bumper stickers studiously, presumably uninterested.

"Had an unaccompanied death down at the Piscatawk View Inn," Ginny explained calmly. "Wife got back from the Bingo Bazaar—that'd be your territory, Dick—and found the body."

"That'll put a kink into the old vacation," Frank commented and went on arranging, humming "What Do You Do with a Drunken Sailor?" a little loudly for Elizabeth's taste.

"Bad luck," Dick agreed. "Shame you guys don't have more summer cops to take some of the strain off you, Gin." He flicked fastidiously at the mosquito guts on his shorts. " 'Course, you don't really *need* them, do you? Not enough tourist traffic to permit the expense."

"We rely solely on police brutality to cut our costs," Ginny murmured. "Wanna see?"

"No, thanks," Dawley demurred. "Word travels. Speaking of which, I heard that Martha Drake is comin' back home for the summ'ah. Is that true, Lizzie?"

Elizabeth wondered how the balloon display had escaped Dick's notice, and then shrugged it off.

"I would tell you," she answered, "but then I'd have to *kill* you. You know how it is with us undercover operatives."

"Oh, you're a riot, Lizzie, just a scream." The mayor of Pebble Beach tucked his pink shirt into his pants, and smiled benevolently. "You just give her my regards, then. She always was the prettiest girl in school. Ya gotta wonder how she held up."

"Ya gotta," Ginny agreed, smacking Dawley's gut pointedly.

He sucked in his belly and said, "Well, I got some leadership responsibilities, so, if you all will forgive me."

Elizabeth stood and swept her hand casually over the surface of the card table before approaching Dawley. Ginny was looking at Dick in that "weighing her options" way that could get dangerous. Elizabeth ran her fingers up the mayor's back and spoke quietly into his ear.

"Remember eighth-grade graduation, Dick?"

"Yeah?" he answered suspiciously. Dick was obnoxious, but almost no one ever said he was stupid. Anymore.

"The dance afterward," Elizabeth prompted. "You remember saying something stupid to me?"

As if he could differentiate, Dick said, "Yeah?"

"And what happened then?" Elizabeth asked.

Dawley paused, sorting out possible responses. Frank jumped into the burgeoning fray, anxious to get on with his work.

"Ginny beat the shit out of you," he answered. "There!" Frank admired his bumper-sticker bonanza. "Go home now, Dick. Your tourist trap needs you."

"Aw, you guys," Dawley blustered. "I better go. There's a traveling carnival setting up on Congress Street. I arranged it special. An elephant, midget clowns, the whole slam. If you close up early—and you just might want to—why don't you come by for a Ferris-wheel ride? It's on me."

"Why not?" Ginny answered and clapped Dick on the back, more gently than he expected.

"All right, then. You bring Martha with you, will ya? Really would like to see her again."

"Good night, Dick," Frank prompted.

" 'Bye," Dick waved and snaked his way through the craft tables and food stalls.

" 'Bye!" Elizabeth, Ginny, and Frank waved at Dick Dawley's back—and a Day-Glo sample of Frank's bumper sticker swaggering away. The "why can't I shoot one?" line read clearly for one hundred yards. Ginny and Elizabeth slapped a high five.

Frank stuck out his hand.

"You owe me five bucks," he told his daughter.

"You owe me a formal wedding," she answered, "so let's call it even."

"Done." Frank gave a last straightening to his goods and started to walk into the crowd. "Could use a good bowl of lobster stew. See you later."

"Ginny?" Elizabeth asked. She pulled a large canvas bag from beneath the table, dumped the toiletries it contained, and released her strawberry blond hair from its band. "Whatever possessed you to move back here to the funny farm after New York City?"

Ginny looked over the paintings and nodded approval as her friend primped. "New York City," she mused. "Not a high enough proportion of nice, clean during-sleep deaths to offset the other, messy kind."

"That's what it was at the Piscatawk View Inn?" Elizabeth handed Ginny a cup of coffee from her thermos, and began applying lip gloss to her mouth.

"Guy was older than God's mother." She sipped. "Doc

Ryan was surprised he even survived the drive up from Boston."

A head of blue hair poked around the corner of the peg-board.

"Now, girls, I believe you know better than to speak ill of the dead. It is not ladylike under any circumstances whatsoever."

"Yes, Miss Locke," the two women answered in unison and then laughed at themselves. Ginny actually blushed from beneath her cropped hair.

"Smoking is neither healthy, nor attractive, and I would recommend just a touch of mascara," Miss Locke continued as she tottered around to look at Elizabeth's paintings. Elizabeth snuffed out her cigarette, though Ginny continued to blow smoke and smile. "That poor man probably smoked. Had he found something more productive to do with his hands, he might still be alive."

Miss Amelia Locke had been both Elizabeth and Ginny's (then Lavinia's) piano teacher, keeping both sets of hands busy practicing from first until eighth grade. Small as a sparrow and straight as a stick, Miss Locke had taught every schoolchild in Dovekey Beach for the past fifty years. Even Frank had learned his musical scales under Miss Locke's tutelage, though he played now only when he was certain there was no one else in the house besides his cocker spaniel, Petunia, the "I-Wonder Dog."

It had been a great relief to Miss Locke to discover that the Will daughters did not display the same personality traits of the father.

Well, Elizabeth did to a certain extent, but for the most part she stifled herself considerably. Avis, of course, was a model of composure and continued to be. Miss Locke waved to Avis as she approached with an unknown man and a familiar woman.

Despite their thirty-two years, Ginny and Elizabeth squealed like two teenagers catching sight of the Beatles.

"Martha Annie!" they screeched together, running toward the street.

Martha Ann Drake was, indeed, still as pretty as the day she was crowned Cod Queen, fifteen years earlier. Tall, ash blond, and so composed and good-natured that no one could hold her beauty against her, Martha launched herself toward her two best friends, through the growing crowd, and away from the handsome man at her side. Avis, too, deserted the tall stranger and toddled behind.

Miss Locke thought in that moment that she had been transported back in time: the three older girls leading, and Avis bringing up an amiable rear. She blushed with pleasure. She had taught every one of them for a varying number of years, and each was a joy in her own right.

Yes, it was a spectacular summer day, all the way around. Miss Locke arranged the sale offerings of the Dovekey Ladies' Guild with satisfaction. Homemade cranberry breads and crocheted toilet-paper covers were tucked between neatly stacked piles of afghan squares, sock monkey dolls, and seashell trinket boxes. The ladies had been especially industrious over the long winter and spring months—and 20 percent of the proceeds went directly to the public library.

Small towns have a way of taking care of themselves.

So far it had not been much of a honeymoon. Marcia had begged for a week in Cancún or at least Miami, but her new husband was not impressed with what he called "gallivanting." Besides, the truck needed a new transmission.

"At least we're here in Dovekey," he reasoned when they arrived the night before, trying to placate his pretty new bride. "You saw. Pebble Beach is tacky, but this is *nice*."

Yeah, yeah, yeah, Marcia griped to herself as she waded into the icy water. B.F.D. The cheap bastard would not even drive an extra seventy-five miles to get to Cape Cod where the Gulf Stream would warm the water enough to swim in without turning French-Canadian blue. B.F.D.

Of all the eligible men in Hazleton, Pennsylvania, she had to marry this cheap bastard.

And she felt like shit, too, not that he cared. It was really too early to be at the beach, but Marcia could not stand the thought of spending another moment in that crappy little room at the bed-and-breakfast watching her new husband snore and drool into the cutesy-poo eyelet sheets. The cheap bastard didn't even spring for a modern hotel room, let alone the bridal suite she had always dreamed of. Marcia's stomach growled like an angry cat. In her righteous snit, she had summarily rejected breakfast (included with bed, of course) except for the somewhat interesting garnish.

She picked an unswallowed piece from between her teeth and was backsided by a wave, her skin exploding in fury of goose bumps.

Frickin' cold. Better to just dive in and get it over with. There sure wasn't any reason to try to save her wedding hairdo; the cheap bastard probably wouldn't even notice if she shaved her head bald.

Besides, the additional misery of the frigid water just might settle her stomach.

Marcia pinched her nostrils determinedly, and pushed herself beneath the surface of the gray blue water just as her bridegroom opened his eyes back in their oh-so-darling room and called for her to come back to bed for a quickie.

Aggressive shouts and the slapping of flesh carried like gunshots over the innocuous sounds of festival preparation.

A horde of large men swarmed the sheep meadow beyond

the festooned common, stripped of their shirts and, in several cases, trousers as well. Elizabeth could just make out a mountain of overdeveloped shoulders glistening in the early-morning shards of sunlight.

"Mary and Joseph!" Elizabeth swore in exasperation. "Avis, go watch my booth, will you?" Avis nodded agreement in the reflexive way of younger sisters worldwide. Elizabeth grabbed Martha's arm and charged off in hot pursuit of Ginny and the melee. The women's reunion would have to wait until the conclusion of whatever police action took place at the sheep meadow.

Normally, Elizabeth found men bashing one another repulsive and unworthy of her feminine attentions, but even from a distance of 200 yards, she had recognized the unclad chest of Dr. Charles MacKay, her other significant pain in the butt.

The canvas duffel bag that lay insidiously in wait for Elizabeth's flashing feet and sent her sprawling indelicately on her face was hurdled delicately by the ever-graceful Martha Drake.

"Hey"—Martha lifted the grass-stained Elizabeth from the mud and plucked a few stray twigs and one small pinecone from her hair—"slow down, or you'll just encourage them."

A communal war whoop reverberated over the manicured lawns. Elizabeth gave the malevolent kit bag a swift kick, then stood on it for a better look at the altercation. Sure enough, MacKay was in the middle of it.

For a man with a Ph.D., Charles MacKay had a nasty habit of leading with his mouth, and for a marine botanist, he had a nastier habit of exhibiting primitive animal behavior. Ginny was used to it by then, but MacKay's baser instincts seemed to infect the general male populace with a profoundly deleterious attitude.

Not that Elizabeth had any intention of interfering on his behalf. This time, it looked as though MacKay was picking on someone—hell, a veritable army of guys—the same size.

She did feel that she owed Ginny some backup, though, and she had a talent in that area. As moderate and sweet-natured as she considered herself, out-of-control males seemed to wither a bit in her presence. Probably due to her years of training with her father. Might as well go with it, she figured.

"Stay here," Elizabeth advised Martha. "I'll be back in a second." She shot off toward the disturbance, and a thundering groan coincided with a resounding smack.

"Uh-huh," Martha answered and ambled behind casually.

Elizabeth spotted Ginny running briskly along the periphery of wasted bodies and into the fray. The chief of police reached the grotesque mass of eight or ten men grappling with one another. One of the smaller brawlers launched himself from a standing position and landed on the backs of three men who appeared to Elizabeth to have been Krazy-Glued together at the shoulders.

Ginny's hand shot skyward. A shrill screech cut through the masculine grunts and profanity.

"*Line out!*" Ginny bellowed and blew her whistle again.

"I knew it." Martha shook her head.

Elizabeth flew to Ginny's side, eyes flashing for signs of danger. Ginny pushed Elizabeth back three feet, keeping her gaze locked on the grimy combatants.

"Off the pitch, Will," Ginny told Elizabeth without turning around.

"What?" Elizabeth asked. "*What?*" she repeated.

"*Off the damned pitch!*" MacKay shouted, backing into her and shifting from foot to foot. "Ref," he yelled at Ginny, "civilians on the pitch!" And pointed at Elizabeth.

Martha Drake pulled Elizabeth to where she had plunked herself down in the moist grass.

"Sit down, Biz."

Elizabeth sat, frowning.

"You're pretty casual, aren't you?" Elizabeth asked Martha. "Isn't that your husband with blood running down his face?"

"It'll stop," Martha answered. She pulled a candy bar from her purse and offered a bite to Elizabeth, who refused. "It always does. Eamon is a world-class clotter."

"*Off side!*" screamed Ginny, throwing a T-shirt to the ground, unbuckling her gun belt and handing it to Elizabeth.

"Oh, *there's* a good reason to marry a man," Elizabeth muttered, wondering exactly what she was supposed to do with a loaded gun.

"Rugby," Martha explained.

Light dawned all over Elizabeth's face. "That is a shitty reason to marry a man."

"Tell me about it," Martha said through a mouthful of chocolate. "Unless, of course, you happen to be an orthopedic surgeon. It's a British Empire sort of thing."

"MacKay isn't British."

"MacKay?"

"My spousal alternative."

"Then he must be Ivy League. Good work, Biz."

"That must be why they call it 'work,' " Elizabeth groused.

"I take it you haven't seen many games."

"Never." Elizabeth took one of the candy bars from the top of Martha's purse and looked at it for a moment with suspicion. "I don't suppose you picked up smoking?" Martha looked at her patiently. "Didn't think so." Elizabeth took a bite and watched a concrete block of a man wearing a large red number three limp off the field, strip off his shirt, and toss it to an even more rectangular male, who trotted back into combat. "How long does this last?"

"How long really, or how long does it *seem?*"

"How long *really*. I'm trying to stay on an earth schedule this year."

"In 'fifteens'; each half is forty-five minutes."

"What if a player dies?"

"Silly girl. They just play around the body."

"Of course. Martha, I have to get back to my paintings. Can you come with me, or are you needed here to suture the players?"

"Not necessary. Eamon has already clotted, see?" Sure enough, he had. "Which one is yours? No, let me guess." Martha inclined her head, as though she were studying a piece of art. "Number eight."

"You know me so well."

"Nah. He's the one who looks most like your dad." Elizabeth cringed, but did not deign to respond to such idiocy. Martha continued. "By the way, how is your Big Frank?"

"Compared to plague or locusts?" Elizabeth stood up, shook her head one last time, and waved Ginny's gun belt in the air. The whistle screamed.

"Penalty, Piscatawk!" Ginny grabbed her holster and handed it to Mr. Elwell, the junior-high-school gym teacher and summer rent-a-cop.

When Elizabeth and Martha got back to the festival stand, Avis was sitting at the card table, hands folded neatly in front of herself.

"Any business?" Elizabeth asked.

"Well," Avis rose, "the bumper stickers are selling like hotcakes and I think someone stole one of your matted wildflower paintings; but you'd better check."

Miss Locke poked around the corner of the display.

"It was some woman from New York City wearing entirely too much makeup." She handed Elizabeth a five-dollar bill. "I saw the ill-gotten gains in her bag, so I overcharged her for a jar of my rose-hip jelly." She smiled sweetly. "The wages of sin, you know."

The wagging of her finger was implied.

"Miss Locke! You look exactly the same!" Martha exclaimed.

"Well, Martha Ann Drake, so do you, except perhaps even a tad bit lovelier, if that could be possible. How this town has missed you and your parents!"

Martha blushed prettily. "I'm married now, Miss Locke. My name is Robson."

"Well, of course you're married," Miss Locke patted the young woman's arm, "how could you *not* be after all these years out in the world?"

How, indeed, thought the radiantly unmarried Elizabeth.

"I've missed home, though," Martha said. "That's why I wanted to be here in the States for Independence week."

Miss Locke searched her memory for the precise relocation of the Drake clan, but could only remember the general gist. "But Canada is very lovely. Quite clean, I'm told."

"That it is. It's well, Canada is so, well, *new*. Western Canada, anyway. I miss winding streets, and cobblestones. I am really looking forward to reacquainting myself. And introducing Eamon to my roots."

"Where are you and your husband staying, dear?" Miss Locke asked.

Elizabeth searched her memory for a recollection of the last time she had vacuumed or changed the sheets.

Avis immediately felt guilty for having three children taking up so much space at her house.

"With Dad and me," Elizabeth offered, throwing caution and her pride to the wind. Frank Will thought of flooring as a giant horizontal magazine rack, and Elizabeth—not much better—used her personal areas as an extension of closet space and laundry facilities. In fact, Petunia the dog was probably the neatest creature in the antique Cape Cod that sat behind the Will art gallery, and she was incontinent periodically.

"We couldn't impose," Martha answered, just as she was trained to.

Elizabeth morosely prepared herself to insist. It was the well-bred thing to do.

Fortunately, Miss Locke was better bred than the Queen of England. "Now, if Elizabeth wouldn't mind terribly, my sister and I would love to have you stay with us. You couldn't know this, Martha Ann, but we've converted that musty old house we inherited into a bed-and-breakfast, and it would be no trouble at all for us to add two more people to our little family."

Always helpful, Avis chimed in, "But it's the height of the season! I thought your rooms were all sold out." Elizabeth wondered briefly why she had ever let her baby sister out of the closet she had locked her in when she was twelve.

"Oh, we are," said Miss Locke, "but we always keep our parents' room available for our friends. It just never seemed right to reduce Mother's and Father's room to a tawdry business venture. It would be such a pleasure to have you."

And if the glow on Miss Locke's aged face were any indication, there could, indeed, not have been anything in the world that would have given her more happiness. She was so radiant, in fact, that Avis forgave herself her fecundity, and Elizabeth promised herself to tidy later in the week.

If nothing truly earth-shattering came up.

But the earth shatters occasionally, even in Dovekey Beach, New Hampshire.

Maybe especially there.

TWO

DUSK WAS PUSHED beneath the ocean's horizon by the implacable weight of evening. The white Victorian "cottage" grayed in the dimming light. Twenty-two rooms napped briefly before a light here and there snapped one at a time into wakefulness. Miss Locke's spidery hand found the ornate brass light switch at the end of the long corridor.

The circular room filled the top of the round tower. Even the wainscoting swirled like a ballroom dancer's skirt against the delicately flowered walls. Three windows glowed with the magic light that always shone from the sea, no matter the darkness of the night.

A master ship's cabinetmaker had fitted a curved window seat beneath the tall leaded panes. Each panel below the tapestry cushioning concealed a spring-latched cubby. Equally amazing was the workmanship of the graceful wardrobe that hugged the swoop of the room, flanked by floor-to-ceiling bookcases.

The bed was of the same vintage as the home itself—high Victorian; forest green cast iron finials of winding leaves and burgundy grape clusters that lent the room an air of indefinable movement, mimicking the washing of the waves below. Heavy brass sconces glowed, their ornateness nearly lost in the rococo pattern of the wallpaper. On the mahogany pie crust table was placed a willowware compote of fresh potpourri and two silver candlesticks sporting bayberry candles.

Martha Ann Drake Robson's eyes filled with tears. Her lips parted to pay appropriate—if that were possible—compliments, but failed.

Elizabeth Will had every intention of filling the quiet, but ended up having a reflex cry with her friend instead. Eamon Robson inspected the cabinetry with wonder (and Elizabeth suspected, discretion), leaving Miss Locke to deal with all the emotion.

"Now, girls," she said, pulling a lace hankie from her pocket and handing it to Martha.

Elizabeth chose to assume that Miss Locke would expect her to have one in a pocket somewhere, rather than that the old woman still liked Martha better.

"It's so . . ." Martha began.

"Beautiful," Elizabeth finished. The two younger women looked at one another and laughed at themselves.

"Yes," Miss Drake agreed, as though viewing someone else's property. "Yes, it is one of the most beautiful rooms I've ever seen, and there used to be so many more of them here in Dovekey before, well, heating costs and so forth. Rose and I close off this whole wing in the winter, but we are very grateful to have it. And"—she pulled an intricate quilt from the blanket chest at the foot of the bed—"we are very grateful to have you young people enjoy it while you're here." She placed the quilt catty-corner on the end of the mattress, just so.

Eamon Robson joined his wife at the doorway and put an arm around her, the way men do with wives in long, pleasant marriages.

"I can see why you get so homesick, Marty. This is a whole 'nother world here."

Elizabeth could well imagine. When Martha's parents had taken her off to Calgary, Alberta, right after graduation, Elizabeth had to look it up in a battered old atlas her father kept in the living room. Further research revealed that Calgary was world-renowned for its rodeo.

Needless to say, to a seventeen-year-old, that did not seem like much of a reason to break up the three closest friends to ever grow up in New England. Ginny and Elizabeth went off to the University of New Hampshire shaking their heads in disbelief. Martha's father was a far cry from a cowboy, and her mother did not have an ounce of pioneering spirit that anyone in the Ladies' Guild had ever noticed. But that was water under the Memorial Bridge, as they say.

Eamon and Martha Robson had been living north of Edmonton, Alberta for the past ten years. Elizabeth had never personally made it farther north nor west than Toronto, but knew enough of British Canada to know she knew, okay, nothing about it, except it all looked dishearteningly new. All very, very tidy.

She could only suppose that as the air got cleaner nearer the Rockies, so did the people. Eamon Robson appeared to be a paragon of squeaky clean. A vision of John Denver passed through her mind and was immediately (almost) dismissed as completely unfair to Elizabeth's friend-in-law.

Elizabeth had a secondary moment's flash of—she admitted it—jealousy. After the knee-jerk categorization of Eamon as profoundly sanitized, she had to confess that her high-school friend had found herself a nearly ideal mate. Eamon was attentive, educated, handsome, and stable to the point of (by Dovekey standards) the macabre. Perhaps Elizabeth had begun to stagnate a little in the bog of history and tradition. Or, what worried her more, she considered the possibility that she had fallen heir to the family's congenital intractability.

Nahhh.

She shook off the implication of genetic doom. Happiness just gave New Englanders the creeps, and the contentment and personal centeredness of the couple, in the same room with Miss Locke, was simply overloading Elizabeth's seriously jaded system.

And not for the thousandth time, Elizabeth wondered about all the things she was and did that gave *herself* the creeps: thirty-something, baby-sitting her nutzoid father instead of her own warped children, lobster fishing like a man, and painting like a society matron.

"Speaking of which . . . " Elizabeth spoke aloud, startling herself a bit.

"What, dear?" Miss Locke asked.

"Sorry,"—Elizabeth checked her waterproof stainless-steel watch—"but I have to get over to the Art Association for tonight's opening. As it is, I left Sandy with all the setup."

"Sandy?" Eamon asked, lifting a brocade pullman onto the blanket chest.

"Ginny's—" Elizabeth started.

"—and Elizabeth's new friend," Miss Locke finished without taking a beat. "A very talented sculptress."

If Martha was relieved by Miss Locke's Amy Vanderbilt–style intervention, she did not show it. Elizabeth blushed at the thought that she had been teetering on the cliff of potential social ineptitude. She did not know whether or not Ginny had ever written Martha about her alternative lifestyle. She could not even remember whether or not she, herself, had told her. Oh, well.

Even if Eamon Robson was as perfectly politically correct as he seemed, the intricacies of Dovekey Beach's sundry variations on the theme of sexual orientation might best be revealed to a newcomer in snippets.

"It would be terrific if you guys are up to an appearance. Dad will be there, like it or not," said Elizabeth.

"I *love* your dad! He's so colorful." Martha exclaimed. "Will your mom be there, too?"

"Well, that's a long story."

Martha squeezed Eamon's arm. It was the arm that, according to Charles MacKay, had gotten "cleated up a little" during the morning's rugby match, and Eamon winced slightly. His wife seemed not to notice, though Elizabeth's forehead crinkled up empathetically.

"A *romance* story!" Miss Locke enthused. "Innocently, of course," she amended. "Mrs. Will has become quite a novelist."

"You're kidding!" Martha obviously believed every word. Sal Will had always been something of the Joan Collins of Dovekey Beach.

"She travels quite a bit these days, doesn't she, Elizabeth?" Miss Locke asked.

"She does, indeed," agreed Elizabeth, still trying to remember whether Sal were in the Czech Republic, Bosnia, or Boston, creating thousands of pages of heaving bosoms and studs with secrets. Elizabeth was not willing to admit to being jealous of her own mother—not even to herself. "Anyway, you know where the association building is, Martha. If you can come, that would be great."

"Are you coming, Miss Locke?" Martha asked.

"Of course," she nodded. "Rose is the president of the association, after all."

"Who's Rose?" Eamon asked.

"I gotta go," Elizabeth said. "See you later, then."

"You bet," Martha said with another innocently sadistic arm clutch.

"I'll find my way out, Miss Locke," Elizabeth tossed over her shoulder and was promptly swallowed into the dim hallways of the huge house. Fortunately, there were only three stairwells and all the doors except those leading to the common rooms were locked, so Elizabeth did not wander aimlessly for more than five or six minutes before finding herself in the kitchen and to the side door leading to the herb garden.

The previously homey kitchen had been modified to accommodate the requirements of a commercial bed-and-breakfast business. Necessary, Elizabeth knew, but sad. From all the glasses of water she had gotten herself during her sister's piano lessons, Elizabeth had always felt as comfortable here as she did in her own home.

Twenty years earlier, the main ceiling rafter hung with dozens of bunches of flowers, strung faces to the floor to dry for arrangements into wreaths and centerpieces. The greenery and bouquets, once everywhere, were relegated to one corner; gay, but so much less than they had once been.

Now, boxes of cold cereal in single-serving sizes glared down from the glass-paned cabinets, and industrial-sized stainless-steel pots dwarfed the 1940s propane stove. The old gold-rimmed Haviland china had been put away for safekeeping and replaced by stacks of plain white ironstone dishware. Commercial trays were already set up for the breakfast rush, each with a bud vase, place settings rolled into damask napkins, and a tourist-sized jar of Miss Locke's famous rose-hip jelly.

Though tempted, Elizabeth could not bear to peek into what had once been a wax museum of a formal dining room. Besides, she was late.

In ways she could not even imagine.

Tethered in an underwater field of undulating seaweed, the cadaver swayed in time with the waves. A small school of pollack nipped at the sodden clothing, but found nothing of interest to eat there. The hatchlings frolicked in and out of the medium-length swirling hair, and nibbled at the algae that had already started to establish a colony near the scalp.

The bottom feeders would remain indifferent to their new visitor until the body sank.

And, should it rise, the gulls would be available for clean up.

The corpse swayed gently.

Elizabeth's 1964 MGB roared into the gravel parking lot of the Dovekey Art Association. Its terminally ill exhaust system announced her arrival with coughs and a final shudder. There were already two trucks and three cars pulled up to the railroad ties that marked the perimeter of the lot. Lights blazed from the tall windows of the old Grange Hall and the double doors stood open and at attention.

Damn, damn, damn! Elizabeth slammed the rusty car door and nearly ripped her long dress off her body before realizing that she had slammed her hem into it as well. *Well, by hell, DAMN!* It was her favorite gallery-opening evening gown: very Jean Harlow, ivory, and slinky.

Sandy hung out the open center window on the second floor and yelled, "*Biz!* Stop fooling around and get your butt up here!"

Overhead, the previously innocuous cover of clouds ripped a seam and let loose a blanket of rain.

"Nice talk," Elizabeth muttered and extricated herself. The MGB's grimy white door screamed in protest and would not re-latch, which made the convertible top sit askew. She kicked the existent dent she had pounded in the side of the car over years of recalcitrant behavior, grabbed up her now-grease-stained hem and shot into the building.

Rain drizzled down her bare back and left dark blotches in the raw silk. Elizabeth reminded herself never again to dress up.

God would only get her for it.

Inside, the second floor was transformed from meeting-room-cum-square-dance studio into a real exhibition hall. The turn-of-the-century upright piano had been rolled to a position diagonal to the far left corner, where Claire Wallis would be banging out background music throughout the evening.

A long folding table had been camouflaged with a white damask cloth, which Elizabeth immediately recognized as a match for the napkins at the bed and breakfast. Rose Locke Sykes was nowhere to be seen, but had left her inimitable mark.

Avis was hanging the last of Elizabeth's watercolors and squinting at the title and price cards in her left hand. As usual, Avis had miscalculated the term "eye height." The frames were all about three or four inches higher than they ought to be, but Elizabeth figured that beggars ought not to be choosers. Besides, in a way, she was commending herself for being unavailable for the hard labor for a change. Frank sat in a folding chair in the center of the room, directing. His pockets bulged with bumper stickers.

"Frank," Mrs. Sykes called from the door to the kitchen area, "get in here and help me carry out the refreshments." She waved—more of a salute, really—to Elizabeth and held the door for Frank. Younger than her sister, Rose Sykes still commanded the ranks like a marine sergeant. Unlike the demure Miss Locke, Mrs. Sykes had also assiduously avoided the blue-hair syndrome of later years and allowed her hair to gray naturally. She was short, but not small; cultured, but blunt. As a junior-high-school teacher, she had scared the crap out her students and still did.

"All right, girly-girl," Sandy barked from behind an eight-foot-tall free-form sculpture, "put some muscle behind this baby so I can get the overview."

"Which direction?"

"Toward me."

"Well, it's about time," Avis grumped, blowing hair out of her eyes and straightening a painting, "I have no idea which label goes with which painting."

Elizabeth squatted inelegantly in her silk dress and pushed at the base of the sculpture.

"*Nubble Light* goes under the painting of Nubble Light. *Advection Fog* goes with the foggy one. *Starry Night* goes with the Van Gogh."

"Very funny!" Avis took a position next to her sister to push.

"Two more inches!" called Sandy. The women grunted and the teetering object slid.

"What did you make this out of?" Elizabeth asked. "Old transmissions?"

Sandy rose to her full height and surveyed the statue's position in the center of the room, frowned, and moved Frank's chair to a corner. "Surely," she said, "that old rust bucket you're driving would be honored to find a peaceable end."

"Ha!" Elizabeth said without amusement. Turning to her sister, she asked, "Where's your husband, anyway? Aside from fathering children, he must be good for some heavy lifting."

"He's baby-sitting. Besides, I had to spend the last minute picking strawberries for your gallery theme."

"Strawberries and champagne are traditional," Sandy said, brushing rust and plaster from her jeans.

"Good strawberries and cheap champagne," Elizabeth corrected. "You *are* going to change, aren't you?"

Frank reentered, carrying two large crystal bowls of ripe berries.

"Women always promise not to, but they always do," he muttered.

"Frank!" Mrs. Sykes called from the kitchen.

"I rest my case," Frank grunted, placing the bowls carefully at opposite ends of the refreshment table and examining the effect. He moved one slightly toward the center.

"Frank Will, get yourself in here! The ice is melting!"

"Coming, Mrs. Sykes."

"I have a dress downstairs in the ladies' room, Biz." Sandy looped her long hair into a ball at the top of her head and shoved a pencil in it to hold it in place. "And exactly how cheap *is* the champagne? And where the hell is Ginny? She promised she'd help me get set up and keep Frank busy. If it hadn't been for Avis, I would have lost my mind."

"You'd better check again, then."

Avis smacked her sister on the arm, leaving a red spot.

"Hey!"

"Hey!"

Mrs. Sykes kicked open the kitchen door. She was carrying a case of bubbly.

"You girls stop that right this instant. Elizabeth," she hoisted the heavy case forward, "take this and ice it properly. *Frank!* Where is that ice? Heaven knows you haven't pulled your weight here this afternoon."

A shot of guilt slammed Elizabeth in the gut as she ran to relieve her old teacher of the heavy bottles. Years of pulling lobster traps had made her strong as a man, for which she was gratified momentarily.

"You're getting a little buff, there, Biz," Avis commented, pointing to the rippling muscles in her sister's back.

"Nothing genteel about tourist season, Avis."

Frank hoisted a large aluminum washbasin filled with ice onto the food table, moving flower arrangements to either side to complete the picture.

"Very nice, Franklin," Mrs. Sykes complimented him. "Now pluck the bumper stickers out of the gladioli and go outside to direct parking. I hear at least six cars pulling in right now."

Nothing wrong with the old lady's hearing.

Frank heaved a sigh of the long-suffering and misunderstood, and shuffled down the stairs with a massive yellow flashlight. Avis removed the bumper stickers as Elizabeth ran to affix the labels to the paintings.

The crowd she did not really expect was arriving early. Probably the rain was driving everyone with an ounce of sanity inside.

Elizabeth smiled as a crack of thunder rattled the windows. Dick Dawley's carnival would not be much of a blockbuster in a whipping summer storm.

She hoped, though not overly ardently, that the Ferris wheel was well grounded.

Within one half-hour, it became obvious that, Edison-approved electrical equipment or no, the Pebble Beach extravaganza had deteriorated into a total—the more imaginative of the commentators excused themselves—washout. As there were no other activities planned for the evening, the Dovekey Beach Art Association scored a major coup.

The unexpected influx of soggy tourists showed Frank to his best advantage: a bureaucratic gift for the rationing of cheap champagne and fresh strawberries. Naturally, anyone purchasing a bumper sticker received preferential treatment regarding seconds.

Sandy was thrilled at making her first sale ever to a nonrelative and in danger of becoming perky.

"Look at this turnout!" she enthused to Elizabeth.

"It feels like a barn in here," Elizabeth answered, even though she wanted to enjoy her transient popularity as much as Sandy was. "All these wet bodies sending off heat. I feel like a tree fungus. And where is Ginny?"

Sandy nodded regally to a singularly fat man in a floral shirt who was inspecting a sculpture titled *Atlantis Swallowed*. Hope sprang eternal.

"Right now, I'd rather know where our pianist is. It sounds all clunky in here."

"I doubt the acoustics would improve with Claire's playing." Elizabeth drained her plastic goblet of champagne.

"Oh, you're just pissed because Claire's dating your father." Sandy handed the tourist in the shirt a brochure of her finest unsold work.

"My father"—Elizabeth took possession of Sandy's half-filled glass and polished it off—"does not *date*." The glass was refitted into Sandy's hand. "Dat*ed,* perhaps."

"Oh, whatever," Sandy conceded, watching Mrs. Sykes take money at the cashier stand, and issue red dots marked with the buyer's name to be applied to the sold items. In logical fashion, she had concluded that most of the patrons would prefer to pick up their valuable buys *après le déluge*. "Oh, look. There's Ginny and your two friends. I guess they made it, after all."

Elizabeth cheered up and waved across the room. Her friends would take her mind off all the money she was, for a change, making. In some social circles, enthusiasm for one's own success is not considered an attribute.

"Hey!" she called.

Ginny worked her way through the crowd, making room in her wake for Martha and Eamon. She gave Sandy a perfunctory hug and patted Elizabeth's cheek as she examined the throng.

"Sorry we're late," Martha said, "but Ginny ended up giving us a ride, anyway, so blame her." She fingered the New Hampshire state flag at the door.

"So *that*'s where you've been," Sandy chided, "hanging out at the Wild Rose instead of getting dirty with the rest of us working stiffs."

Elizabeth noticed Eamon flush.

"Bad word," Martha said. "The reason we all came together is that Ginny was investigating the disappearance of a young woman staying at the Wild Rose. She was on her honeymoon, and her husband is frantic."

"That's a word for it," Ginny commented. "Men get so testy when they're stood up." She headed toward a tray of freshly filled glasses on the table next to Mrs. Sykes. Apparently, Frank had decided that anyone coughing up cash should get further refreshment.

"You don't look too worried," Elizabeth said and handed the threesome their own glasses, and another for herself.

"About what?" asked Rose Sykes.

Ginny lit a cigarette; Mrs. Sykes pushed the standing ashtray in her direction.

"One of your guests took a hike sometime this morning and doesn't seem to want to be found."

The color under the liberal application of blusher left Mrs. Sykes's face.

"Who?" Her frown showed the same mixture of concern and irritation the young women remembered very well from seventh-grade geography class.

"Genetti."

"I don't believe it," Mrs. Sykes said and took a sip of cider. "He was so conscientious. So attentive." Her brow crinkled.

"Nuh-uh"—Ginny shook her head—"it was the wife."

Mrs. Sykes relaxed visibly. "Oh, then I wouldn't worry too much, right away. The bride was"—a thesaurus flashed across her powdered face—"being somewhat petulant. I don't believe she was getting the honeymoon she had expected. Surely Amelia must have mentioned it. We had to ask them to keep their discussion down a bit last night. Our other guests were complaining."

Ginny exhaled smoke. "Miss Locke mentioned it." Ginny

gave a near-smile. "So did the other guests. Still"—she looked down the stairwell toward the sound of heavy feet—"the groom looks pretty unhappy. His new in-laws haven't heard from her. But you're right—she's probably just off having a snit and punishing him for something or another."

As they neared, anonymous footsteps slowed in conjunction with a distinct wheezing pattern.

The Chief of Police launched an overdue ash directly into the chest of a wet and winded Dick Dawley.

"Hey, Gin, watch it! Don't you guys have any smoking regulations in this town?"

"Private property, Dick." Ginny stubbed out the cigarette, blowing her last lungful of smoke into his face. "And what brings you here to our little hamlet?"

"Oh, you know. Curiosity. Fellowship."

"And the carnival split early." Ginny elbowed Elizabeth, who grinned openly. "With quite a few wallets."

"You mean," Elizabeth asked, wide-eyed, and with a feigned incredulity that would do her father justice, "there was a criminal element amongst the traveling folk?"

"Oh, just shut up, Biz," Dawley said.

Mrs. Sykes perked up.

"You watch your tongue there, Mr. Dawley. You are speaking in the presence of ladies."

Mr. Dawley fairly bit off his tongue and its response.

"Sorry," he muttered, then rallied. "How did you get word so fast, Gin? It hasn't exactly been on Channel Nine yet."

"Police scanner, Dick." Ginny shook her head at the denseness of certain public officials.

"Duhh." Elizabeth groaned and led Martha and Eamon into the fray of the lively art exhibit. Ginny and Sandy followed without a backward glance.

Dawley watched the exodus, his brow furrowing.

"Was that Marty Drake?" he asked.

"She still is, Richard," Mrs. Sykes answered reflexively. "She is not, as yet, deceased."

There was a short beat for information processing.

"Oh, yeah. Right."

Carrying what appeared in the flashes of lightning to be a picnic basket, the dark figure scrabbled over the granite boulders that formed the seawall at the new State Beach. A nondescript American car was parked at the crest of a rise and twist in the beach road, making it nearly impossible to see between spikes of lightning.

With practiced coordination, the unlikely picnicker shuttled over the barrier and disappeared from sight into a wall of driving rain and onto the gray granite sand.

It was often said in Dovekey that heavy doses of ozone during a thunderstorm made folks wicked peculiar.

As usual, a Yankee understatement.

THREE

MICA IN THE blacktop of the beach road flickered in the bright summer sun, as though the meandering two-lanes had been sprinkled with fairy dust. The cedar-shake cottage that served as the Elizabeth Will Gallery was open and welcoming to the cool breeze that wafted from the ocean across the street. Martha Robson stood at the seawall and breathed deeply while her husband helped Elizabeth and Avis unload paintings from the back of Avis's black Jeep.

Eamon Robson stole glances at his wife's back with every trip in or out. Elizabeth coveted the attention. Dr. Charles MacKay, her particular spousal alternative, was out on his island laboratory analyzing samples of God-only-knew what for God-only-knew who. It would never occur to him that she might need help moving stock from last night's art opening back to her business.

Not that she resented it.

Frank wasn't available for any heavy lifting, either.

Elizabeth told herself she was used to it.

"Couldn't you switch to painting stuff that doesn't need

glass in the frames?" Avis complained. Eamon lifted the largest of the unsold watercolors from the night before from Avis's hands, double-checked his immobile wife, and wondered what could be holding her in such a trance. As though she sensed his attention, she turned and waved.

Eamon's face broke into a brilliant smile. As Martha started back toward the gallery, on her behalf, Eamon checked both directions for oncoming traffic and walked toward the shoulder to wait for her.

Avis filled Elizabeth's arms with portfolios of matted pieces. She took them, but made no move.

"Nice, isn't it?" Avis asked, nodding to Martha and Eamon.

"Nice," Elizabeth said, "is a nice word."

"You're jealous," Avis pulled the last of the art out of the Jeep. "You always were, a little."

"Am not."

"Are, too."

"No, suh."

"Yes, suh. That's why you used to pick on her."

"Did not."

"Did, too. You wanted to be class president and pageant queen. You were just too lazy." Since Avis's statement was true, Elizabeth did not bother to argue the point. "It's nice to have someone care that much about you."

"There's that 'n' word again," Elizabeth said and turned into the doorway of the gallery.

"Needed is another 'n' word." Avis followed her sister and left the happy couple to themselves.

"I'm needed," Elizabeth grunted and lifted her load onto the framing table. She hated it when her sister was right. As the elder, she doggedly asserted her right not to admit it, though. "If it weren't for me during that spring blizzard, MacKay would never have gotten pushed out of that ditch."

"Oh, wow. A gentleman would have let you drive instead of push."

"Yeah, yeah"—Elizabeth lifted an especially pricey painting to the pegboard—"and a real man wouldn't drive an automatic."

"Now you sound like Dad."

"Do not."

"Do so."

"No, suh."

"Yes, suh."

"Knock it off, you two, or I'm grounding you, Elizabeth," Frank ordered.

"I should be so lucky," she answered. "I notice you always ground me *after* we've pulled the lobster traps."

"Your Gramma Will didn't raise any 'idyuts.' "

Eamon delivered his painting, setting it against the wall by the doorway and putting his arm around Martha.

"Is that it?" he asked.

Frank searched the pockets of his khaki pants and pulled out a piece of war-torn yellow paper.

"You two look kinda peaked-like. Touristy." Frank gave the crumpled wad to Eamon. "Thought you might like to get some sun whilst we have it. That there's a permit to the town beach, so you don't have to go sittin' around with a mess of massholes and New York-uhs at the state park." Frank sat, thoroughly pleased with himself, in one of the bentwood chairs in the far corner to watch his daughters put the gallery back in order. "Elizabeth will work you to death, if you don't watch her."

Elizabeth and Avis sighed in unison.

"Eamon doesn't mind." Martha hugged him closer.

"No doubt his parents drug him up good and proper," Frank continued, "but you two are pastier than a piecrust, so git."

Eamon wore the poker face of a man who has found an exit,

but doesn't want to give himself away. Elizabeth knew that Charles MacKay would already have been spreading his blanket and sucking up the rays.

Not that it bothered her.

She hefted the heavy frame from the floor and heaved it into position at eye level. It was so weighty that it took two hangers to be safe. She wondered what it would be like to be loved, and cared for, a fussed-over and—

—she dropped the painting. Glass shards flew through the dappled lighting and across the moss green carpeting. Miraculously, no one was cut, except of course, Elizabeth. Tiny slivers of glass stuck in a spray down one bare leg, drizzling blood.

"Shit!"

"Nice talk," Frank commented. Avis was already traveling to the back room, where the medical supplies were kept.

"Are you all right?" Martha asked.

Eamon was immediately at Elizabeth's side.

"You'd better let me look at that." He squatted. "I'm pretty good with these things."

Probably pretty good at damned near everything, thought Elizabeth with no particular pleasure. Marriage, work, even pissant, who-gives-a-rat's-ass rugby. There was no doubt in Elizabeth's mind.

She was getting a crush on her friend's husband. She looked at the muscles in his shoulders rippling under his white cotton T-shirt as he dabbed at the blood running down her leg. It was more than a crush.

Elizabeth wanted Eamon Robson in the worst way—and that would be any way at all. Maybe it showed, or sent off some sort of pheromone stink or something, because Martha displaced her husband and took over clean-up duty.

"You know," she said to Eamon, "Mr. Will is right. I think a day at the beach would give you some color and let you unwind from the long trip." She carefully tweezed two of the larger pieces of glass from Elizabeth's shin. The care with which she did it sent a pang of guilt to Elizabeth's stomach. "I'd like to hang around here, though, and catch up on girl stuff. You don't mind, do you?"

"Of course not," he answered.

Of course not, Elizabeth whined to herself. Eamon Robson was the kind of man who always remembers to put down the toilet seat. Understanding, too, may he burn in hell.

"Thanks for understanding, honey." Martha stood up and kissed him. "You know how to get back to the Wild Rose—right down the beach road and your first right. Miss Locke or Mrs. Sykes will point you to the town beach. Biz or Avis can shuttle me around."

"Okay, darling." He kissed Martha sweetly and squeezed Elizabeth's arm. "You all right?" Elizabeth nodded, too green with envy to speak. "All right, then. I'm off. See you all at dinner tonight."

"Probably won't recognize you for your mahogany tan," Frank said. "I'll keep the girls out of trouble whilst you're un-laxing."

That'll be the day, Elizabeth and Avis thought as though they were joined unnaturally at the brain stem.

As Eamon pulled his rental car carefully onto the beach road and drove off in the proper direction at the precise speed limit, Ginny Philbrick parked the Dovekey Beach police cruiser in his vacated spot. Eamon stuck his left arm out the window and waved farewell from down the road.

Elizabeth and Martha wandered over to the police car while Avis tried to deal with the insurmountable difficulties of splintered glass in carpet, and her father.

"Where's Eamon off to without the little woman?" Ginny asked.

"To get some R and R on the town beach," Elizabeth answered.

Martha looked troubled.

"He has someone else's town-beach pass. That won't be a problem will it, Gin?"

"Only if Mr. Elwell believes he really is Frank," Ginny answered, as aware of Frank's petty anarchistic proclivities as everyone else in town. "As far as I know, Frank has never set foot on the beach, except to set off illegal fireworks."

"I know it's silly, but I wouldn't want Eamon to get into any trouble here in the States." Martha appeared visibly relieved.

"Rest easy, Marty," Ginny said, "this is New Hampshire, not Nicaragua." There was a blat from the cruiser radio. Just as Ginny reached for the door handle, the radio crackled again, and Mr. Elwell's voice came across loud and clear.

"Ginny? Come in, heah, Ginny?"

Mr. Elwell was a good teacher, but he had never really gotten the hang of policing.

"Yes. I'm here," Ginny spoke into the mike. She waited for a response that did not come. "What's cookin' Mr. E?"

"Ten-four, Ginny. My location is the Breakfast 'n' Beans. Ten-four?"

The three women stifled giggles. As teenagers, all three had crushes on their (then young) gym teacher. In one another's presence, they were regressing.

"Ten-four, Mr. E. What's happening?"

"An egg boycott, perhaps," Elizabeth observed. "Maybe an undertipping offense by a French-Canadian?"

"Ten-four, Ginny. We have a ten-fifty-two occurring at this location."

"A what?" Ginny clicked off.

"Ten-four, Ginny. Make that a ten-forty-two, I think."

"Spit it out, Mr. E." Ginny released the microphone button. "He doesn't get it," she explained to her friends. "We don't get enough infractions around here to number them."

Martha Robson turned her face to the sun and smiled to herself, just as she had a decade and a half before; and the sun seemed to smile back at her.

"Ten-four, Ginny." The sound of pages being turned came across the radio along with some muttering. "We have a ten-fifty-*four* in progress at this location. Ten-four?"

"A *what*, Mr. E?"

"That would be a fire, Ginny. Ten-four?"

"Ten-four, Mr. E, ten-four. Has the fire department been notified?"

"I don't know, but they're here. Ten-four?"

"I'm on my way," Ginny hung up the mike, picked it up again, and said, "Over and out."

"That's a ten-four," Mr. Elwell got the final word.

"Will the excitement never end?" Ginny asked herself. "Sorry, guys, but I'd better get over there before they start toasting the marshmallows. Wanna take a look?"

"Sure!" Martha chirped, sliding gracefully into the back of the cruiser.

"Avis!" Elizabeth called into the doorway. "Mind the store for a while, will you?" And without waiting for what was certain to be acquiescence, Elizabeth got into the front seat next to Ginny. "Can we turn on the siren?"

"And the blue light?" Martha added. "I haven't been involved in a police action since, well, never."

"What the hell," Ginny answered, flipping two switches and racing down the beach road, scaring the vinegar out of several cars with out-of-state plates and small vacation stashes of recreational pharmaceuticals. Ginny Philbrick loved her job.

As reported, the volunteer fire-and-rescue corps was on the scene. Smoke poured from the back window of the popular local restaurant at about the same rate that the populace with police scanners poured from their cars for a little titillation.

Stuffed like sausages into their matching royal blue polyester jumpsuits, Asa and Maggie Fleck were shooing away nonexistent paramedic groupies from the newly washed ambulance.

Vinnie Bartlett, the owner of the glorified coffee shop, was wringing his hands by the deserted fire truck.

Elizabeth could see through the double picture windows that Rollie and Terri Ouimet were assiduously finishing their breakfasts. Waste not, want not. Platitude number 4,652.

The air looked a bit funky in the dining room, but not much worse than it would if there were a dozen smokers hanging out over coffee. Mr. Elwell was standing in the middle of the road directing traffic, though it wasn't really necessary: Every car that approached pulled over to catch the action, anyway.

"What's up, Vinnie?" Ginny asked.

"I don't believe it. I just don't believe it," Vinnie ranted. "I just put up new curtains, and now *this! *Brand-new. *White, *no less, by gawd."

"Talk to me, Vinnie. Fire department in there?"

Vinnie nodded miserably. Elizabeth and Martha stepped over the inactive fire hose and followed it from the truck to the back of the building for a better look. Vinnie and Ginny followed. Martha sniffed the air and crinkled up her aquiline nose.

"Smells like a grease fire," she said.

"Imagine that," Elizabeth commented. "Vinnie, have you started using grease in your food preparation?"

"Don't think I require your two-cents'-worth, Missy. Could call your by-gawd father for snotty comments."

"Grease fire," the captain of the fire department announced out the back door to Ginny.

"Just opened my new tourist court, too," Vinnie groused. "Five new cabins within easy walking distance of the beach.

Kitchenettes in two of 'em, and RV hookups off to tha' side. Needed *this* like another belly button." For the first time Vinnie noticed the tall, cool blonde standing with Ginny and Elizabeth.

"Marty? Martha Ann Drake, that you? By gawd, 'tis. And you lookin' as pretty as when you left."

"Thank you, Vinnie." Martha took the older man's hand, which provided the soothing effect of a fistful of Valium. Vinnie's shoulders unscrunched, and he smiled at her, despite his agitation. Ginny clapped Vinnie on the back and peered through the smoke into the kitchen. Elizabeth sat on a garbage can, already bored.

She should have known better than to let down her guard, but she was more fundamentally optimistic than she would ever let on.

"Evacuate!"

The order transmitted over the emergency vehicle's sound system had a hollow science-fiction quality, its annoyance factor surpassed only by its sheer volume level. A spine-splitting squeal followed.

"THIS IS AN EMERGENCY. REPEAT. E-MER-GENCY. OCCUPANTS WITHIN THE IMMEDIATE VICINITY . . . "

Ginny tore past Martha and Elizabeth toward the noise at the front of the beleaguered restaurant.

" . . . ARE INSTRUCTED TO EVACUATE IMMEDI-ATELY."

Asa Fleck sounded as though he were reading his orders off an especially poorly printed cue card.

"PLEASE STRICTLY FOLLOW THE ORDERS OF YOUR EMERGENCY PERSONNEL. DO NOT PANIC. REPEAT . . . "

Elizabeth heard another squeal before she arrived at the

talking ambulance, but it was human rather than technological. Well, it was Asa, anyway.

"Ginny, fo'ah Mike's sake, you justa'bout tore off my fing'ahs."

Ginny held the microphone in her right hand, stretching the coiled cord rhythmically inward and outward, inward and out; the veins stood out in her neck, and her lower jaw jutted forward and rocked back and forth in time with her molestation of the coaxial cable.

Elizabeth unfolded the transmitter from Ginny's hand. The chief of police did not tear her eyes from Asa Fleck who, though considered generally intellectually challenged by his neighbors, had the good sense to rear backward.

"Ginny," Elizabeth soothed, "death by hanging is not legal in this state."

"Elizabeth," Ginny crooned back through clenched teeth, moving closer to Asa, "oh, yes it is."

A contingent of half-dressed tourists spilled from their cabins and RVs. Youngsters mewled, mothers smothered children in bosoms, and fathers barked. The wild-eyed evacuees spread their terror to the erstwhile-bemused locals as the decibel level rose. Ginny reached for the microphone. Elizabeth paused for a moment before relinquishing her possession.

"*False alarm,*" Ginny announced. And when the crowd quieted, she repeated, "False alarm, everybody. The fire is under control. It is confined to the kitchen area and is not threatening any of the outbuildings. Okay?" She surveyed the assembly and nodded to herself.

"Oh, gawd!" Vinnie muttered.

"Coffee for everyone," Ginny added over the public address system, "on Vinnie, as soon as we clear out."

"Oh, gawd!" Vinnie moaned. Public relations was never his

strong suit. On the other hand, neither was cooking, and Vinnie was one of the few tourist-driven businesses that made a profit, year in and year out.

Go figure.

"Where the hell is Maggie?" Ginny asked.

Elizabeth noted the singular lack of response from Asa. Ginny's years on the New York City Police Department were not wasted. She poked Asa's stomach a good one with her forefinger and rephrased the question.

"Where"—she poked again for emphasis—"is your—" a pause—"wife?"

A scream punctured the intensity of the Kodak moment, followed by what was later to be described as a water buffalo in a royal blue jumpsuit heaving itself through the crowd.

It was Maggie, blathering to beat the band.

"I was . . . I was . . . I was . . . " she elaborated.

"And ever shall be," Elizabeth could not resist finishing.

"She's HYPERVENTILATING!" Asa diagnosed sagely. "Somebody get a paper bag. QUICK!"

The melodrama was getting old, and the locals started to thin out. The mall would be opening shortly, and Sears was having a whopper of a sale for the holiday.

Paper bag, indeed.

Elizabeth prayed to God that no one she cared about ever had the double misfortune of a heart attack, or a car accident, or a sinus infection with the Flecks in charge of triage. High-tech paper bag, indeed.

"Sit down, Maggie," Ginny instructed, "and put your head between your knees."

"But I . . . but I . . . but I . . . "

Asa disappeared into the ambulance and fell out the door carrying an oxygen tank and mask.

"Isn't hyperventilation too *much* oxygen?" Martha asked

46

Elizabeth, assuming from old habit that she would know, or at least pretend that she did.

"Ayuh," Elizabeth nodded, figuring that one good shot of a volatile gas would at least put the hysterical paramedic out of Ginny's misery for a few minutes. But Ginny was tough. She cut Asa short with a glance.

"Sit and bend over, Maggie. Now!" It was only the beginning of July, and Ginny needed a vacation. She shoved Maggie down into a sitting position on the sideboard of the ambulance and forced her head down. "Breathe. Slowly."

"I can't tell you how much I've missed home," Martha commented happily. "I don't believe I've had this much fun since the night of the senior prom."

"Always knew you were crazy as a shithouse rat," Elizabeth answered.

Sound came from Maggie's mouth and bounced back up off the parking-lot pavement.

"Duh . . . duh . . . duh . . . "

Ginny leaned forward in order to hear better. "Breathe in and out, slowly, Maggie. We're not going anywhere." More's the pity, she thought to herself.

"Duh . . . duh . . . dead," Maggie gasped.

Asa pushed himself between the police officer and his wife. He pulled a penlight out of the plastic holder in his jumpsuit breast pocket and checked Maggie's pupils.

"You're fine, hon, just fine." He flipped off the light and grasped her wrist, in search of a pulse. "Listen, ya' heah? You're breathin' just fine. Not dead t'all." He tried her other wrist.

Maggie raised her head and stared into her squatting husband's eyes.

"Not me, you damned fool. The tourist in cabin five." Maggie sat up fully and took a lungful of fresh air for the informational launch. "I was checking to make sure we'd evacuated everybody, and there he was, all tucked in and looking for the world like he was sleepin', but t'wasn't. No suh-ree. Deader than Prohibition."

"Oh, shit!" Ginny muttered under her breath and headed to the last cabin at the end of the gravel drive. As she trudged forward with Elizabeth and Martha, Vinnie raced ahead.

"Oh, gawd, not the Governor Wentworth Cabinette," he complained. "It's the diamond in the tourist-court crown." He stopped at the open door. "Full bath, ya know."

Martha Ann put her slender arm around the man's shoulders and moved him aside to allow Ginny and Elizabeth access.

Elizabeth stopped just at the entrance, as much out of shock as to stay out of the way. Ginny walked to the body on the bed which, just as Maggie reported, looked as though he were sleeping peacefully. Ginny pressed her first two fingers to the man's carotid artery, and lowered her ear to his mouth for signs of life.

Nothing.

"As a doornail," Ginny announced.

Elizabeth's eye caught a flash of white. She entered the main and only full room of the cabin and went directly to the ugly-beyond-belief red maple bureau. A pink plastic doily barely camouflaged the water rings in the finish. Elizabeth was not surprised that Vinnie had decorated his new motel empire in early New Hampshire yard sale.

There was a note written on the back of an envelope taped to the bureau mirror. Elizabeth read aloud.

"Gone for a walk on the beach. Will be back before the York outlet stores open. Love, Me."

Ginny shook her head. "Hi, honey, I'm home. Damn, I hate this!" She pulled the bedsheet over the dead man's face. "Damn!" The chief took the envelope from Ginny and turned it over to look for an addressee.

"Sorry, Gin," Elizabeth said. "I'll stay with you for notification, if you want."

"It's okay, Biz. Part of the job." Ginny lit a cigarette for herself and one for Elizabeth. "But it's worse when the deceased is old. Like giving bad news to your own grandmother."

Vinnie hauled himself into the cabin through sheer force of will. The scene on the bed confirmed his fear.

"Why me?" he groaned. "Why is it always me?"

"Fact is, it isn't," Ginny assured him. "This is the second this week. Three, if we don't get some good news about the missing honeymooner."

"I think a corpse in every hotel might be stretching bad luck a bit far, even for Dovekey Beach," Martha said from the doorway. "Like Mrs. Sykes taught us: a chicken in every pot." Platitude number 699.

Elizabeth agreed it was bad politics and worse luck, for whatever it was worth to the harried Vinnie, and then pondered how joyous Martha's yearned-for homecoming was turning out to be. She looked wrung out and pale.

But, then, so did everyone standing vigil in the Governor Wentworth Memorial Cabinette.

The Elizabeth Will Gallery closed for the day, even though it was a Sunday. It was perfect beach weather—an art-business killer—and the coroner's van parked less than a mile away probably would not be particularly inspirational for stimulation of the tourist trade, either.

Frank Will, the Host with the Most, took advantage of the opportunity to fully monopolize Elizabeth's downtime, and invited the Robsons for a lobster dinner back at the little Cape Cod–style house.

"No, no trouble at all." He grinned. "I'll delegate."

Eamon Robson was already back at the Wild Rose Bed-

and-Breakfast when Elizabeth dropped his wife off. In contrast to Martha's pallor, Eamon's fair British skin had burned badly in just an hour of summer sun. Miss Locke had assigned him the task of picking blackberries for an afternoon snack before he dropped off into an inevitable post-beach nap.

Being perfect and all, he went out into the garden without a complaint, though his sunburn virtually radiated misery.

"Martha, maybe you two should just give in to jet lag tonight," Elizabeth suggested. "I'll make lobster-salad sandwiches for tomorrow."

"Oh, sure," Martha said sarcastically. "Like your father has ever left a leftover hanging around in his life. I don't want to miss a single thing."

"We're fine," Eamon agreed. "A little nap and I'll be right as rain."

Elizabeth thought he would be better off to spend the evening encased in Noxzema rather than chowing down with the troops at the house she shared with Frank. But Eamon had insisted, and perfect people get what they deserve.

The price of perfection, Elizabeth thought, is pain, and she drove off to her assigned chores.

As she maneuvered the sharp corner at the State Beach, she was annoyed at a traffic slowdown, and then taken aback.

The ubiquitous Mr. Elwell was again flagging people on by from his station on the solid yellow line of the beach road. Twice in one *day?*

And Elizabeth thought *her* job stank.

She pulled to a stop by Mr. Elwell's side. A Massachusetts driver behind her hit the horn before her brake lights had lit. She ignored it.

"What's going on?" she asked.

"Staties investigating some stuff washed up on the beach." Mr. Elwell ignored the Massachusetts driver, as well, except to hold up his gloved hand to emphasize his ignoring. "It'll be cleared up soon, unless they get all wimpy and New Jersey on us."

"How so?"

"Medical waste." The driver behind Elizabeth honked again. Mr. Elwell reached into his pocket. "No reason to close up the recreational facilities. Happens all the time."

"Not here, it doesn't happen," said Elizabeth, envisioning small children stepping gingerly over biohazard bags and topping their sand castles with festive syringe flags. Another blast of a car horn broke her concentration.

"Nope," Mr. Elwell agreed. "Heard Martha Drake is back in town for a visit. That true?"

"Ayuh. That was her with me at the fire."

"Thought so. Damned if she isn't as pretty as the day she left. How is she doin'?"

Elizabeth waited for the especially long scream of the car horn behind her to cease. "Fine, I guess. There's been a lot of excitement around here. I'll tell her you send your regards."

"I'd 'preciate that. Now move along, Elizabeth. I got a ticket to write for disturbing the peace."

She pulled away as Mr. Elwell marched himself to the car behind her. Medical waste? From where?

Oh, well, she had things to do before dinner.

"I hate this," Avis complained.

"He's your father," Elizabeth responded.

"I hate the water."

"Row!"

"I got married just to avoid this kind of life."

"Good job." Elizabeth grabbed the mooring rope and handed it to her sister. "Any more griping, and I'll make you pull up the pot."

"No, suh."

"*Yes,* suh." Elizabeth located the extra line tied to the mooring about a foot beneath the surface of the water and started to pull. The lobster trap was only two feet down, so it was not much of a job until the slats hit the surface. Then the weight of three pecks of clams started fighting her. "Lean to the left, or we'll both be swimming to shore."

Avis complied. She hated the submarine game.

"I really hate this."

"You don't mind *eating* them." Elizabeth hoisted the trap into the dory, accidentally on purpose sloshing cold salt water from Avis's face to foot.

"You did that on purpose."

"Yes, suh."

"No su—" Avis caught herself. "You're getting more like Dad every day."

"That was a cheap shot, Avis." Elizabeth opened the parlor section of the trap and dumped the clams into a large white plastic bin in the middle of the small wooden boat. The clams had been fed cornmeal for several days, and their bellies had swelled beneath the gray shells as they simultaneously cleaned their systems of sand. Even Avis knew it was worth the trouble. She just complained out of habit.

"Avis?"

"What?"

"You hear anything about a washup of medical waste at the state beach this afternoon?"

"*Our* state beach?"

"No," Elizabeth heaved the empty trap back over the side, and took over the rowing, "the *Nebraska* State Beach."

Avis was too happy to be off-duty to respond to her sister's pervasive sarcasm.

"No, I didn't. Besides, I doubt it. Where would that junk come from?"

"Damned if I know," said Elizabeth. "Might drive some business my way, though, if they don't get the beach open tomorrow for the day-trippers."

"You shouldn't derive pleasure from the discomfort of others," Avis said.

"Oh, shut up, or I'll turn back the gallery-slave duty to you."

Frank whistled "Thirteen Men on a Dead Man's Chest" as he tossed lobsters into the massive pot of boiling water.

"Don't you kill them first?" Eamon asked. He was just about as red as his upcoming dinner.

"That'd be *cruel*," Frank said, and threw a pound of butter into the microwave to melt. "You've been watchin' too much Julia Child, boy. Dead is dead."

Elizabeth hoped Eamon could triumph over his humanitarian scruples before dinner was served. He did not look especially hungry after witnessing the cold-blooded murder of fifteen crustaceans. To be fair, she reminded herself, a killer sunburn has a tendency to make the strongest of men a little nauseous. It was a good thing everyone else at the table was used to dining swathed in the distinctive aroma of Noxzema.

After a slow start, Eamon got over his queasiness and scarfed down as many steamed clams as Frank had—and that was quite a few. There are few foods in the world that look as unappealing as a goopy clam, hanging from its shell. Elizabeth had to admire the inlander for his pluck.

At the end of the meal, both Martha and Eamon were about to fall asleep on their plates, so the requisite poker game was canceled and rescheduled for the next week, when Ginny and Sandy could join in.

Elizabeth delegated, and Avis did the dishes so her sister could walk their guests to their rental car.

Eamon opened the car door for Martha, which she seemed to accept without thought.

Elizabeth tried to remember the last time she had had a car door opened and closed for her, and gave up.

"Tomorrow night, let's all go out to dinner. Ginny and her roommate, too. My treat." Eamon's earnest face was illuminated by the car light. "There's a really quaint restaurant I'd like to try."

Elizabeth thought it took a real man to use the word "quaint" in mixed company.

"Actually, I have a date tomorrow night."

"A Monday-night date?" Martha asked from the passenger seat. "Isn't Saturday night date night?"

Elizabeth reminded herself that Martha never had a mean bone in her body. Nonetheless, she did not want to get into the peculiarities of what passed for her social life.

"Chuck? Bring him along," Eamon offered happily.

Chuck? Right.

She always called him MacKay, illustrating, no doubt, that they had never fully recovered from the adversarial tone of their initial relationship. Chuck, she reasoned, was obviously some sort of rugger-mate nickname.

No one called Charles MacKay "Chuck." His students called him Dr. MacKay. The locals referred to him as the nutburger who lived out at the isles. Frank Will settled on the simple "Biostitute environmental pinhead." She had never heard him called "Chuck."

At least she would be damned if she ever called him anything that cute—the non-car-door-opening environmentalist pinhead.

Still, Elizabeth conceded that Eamon probably needed someone as outside the Dovekey Beach circle as Mackay with whom to bond, and Elizabeth's dating pool was shallow, to say the least.

"Great."

Elizabeth waved Martha and Eamon down the long drive and past the gallery. She hoped there would be some time for a real visit with her friend. Alone.

They had never really had a chance to say good-bye after graduation. The Drakes had packed up two hundred years of village residence and left the country before Elizabeth even had the chance to adjust to the concept of Dovekey Beach without a Drake family.

There was so much to catch up on.

Eamon Robson fell into a deep sleep immediately. Martha was wide awake and antsy, but did not want to disturb her husband by turning on a reading light. Quietly, she unlatched the backstairway door to their room and felt her way down the narrow steps that she knew would lead to the kitchen.

The Drakes' old family home on Whipple Road had the same layout. Martha used to refer to the back stairs as "The Great Escape," however imperfect the categorization. Once the eagle-eyed Claire Wallis moved next door, sneaking out became annoyingly dicey.

Empathetically she hoped Miss Locke and Mrs. Sykes would not mind her helping herself to some milk or tea to get her off to sleep. With any kind of luck, they would have a television in the kitchen. It was about time that Channel 36 went off the air. Martha was in a mood to hear the national anthem played for an occasion other than a hockey game.

The stair treads were no more than six inches deep, and Martha had to place her foot sideways to maintain her balance on the curved decline. At the base of the stairwell, light shone from the kitchen. Martha could barely make out the elderly sisters' quiet conversation from the cracked door. Their voices soothed her.

The plane trip had been long, and the drive up from Logan Airport in Boston harrowing. Eamon had been solicitous, but Martha could feel herself becoming more and more tense, the closer they got to home. She was probably trying to cram too much into too little time. After all, she was no longer the blushing pageant queen.

Like a little girl up past her bedtime, Martha Ann Robson sat in the dark and watched the women making up a batch of Miss Locke's famous wild rose-hip jelly. It took her back to her childhood.

Paraffin melted in a double boiler on the old stove, and the steam from the sterilized canning jars was pulled up the stairway and warmed Martha's bare feet.

Secrets everywhere. Secret stairways, secret recipes.

No reason to disturb the sisters when she was finally feeling so comforted. She watched from beneath half-closed lids for nearly half an hour and then calmly felt her way back up the servants' stairs to the room she shared with her husband.

She remembered the slumber parties from high school, back before there were husbands, when Ginny was still dating boys, before Mrs. Will had run off to Eastern Europe to write paperback novels, when everyone she knew was American.

She had so much to catch up on. It had been so long since she had been home. Looking forward to the next day, Martha fell asleep under Eamon's sunburned and rugby-cleated arm.

Down the hall, a young bridegroom listened to the moan of the lighthouse and cried bitterly for his missing wife.

FOUR

THE OCCUPANTS OF the dining room looked up, if not in horror, then in distaste. The smell was subtle, yet odious.

Elizabeth trailed behind her father, snaking her way through the maze of tables until they reached the Robsons. Eamon frowned, paused in the middle of slathering his second English muffin with rose-hip jelly, and sniffed the air.

Mrs. Sykes, carrying a tray of scrambled eggs and ham, froze in the doorway leading from the kitchen and scowled.

She glared at Frank. "I will bring some fresh coffee while you tidy up."

"I'm sorry," Elizabeth stuttered.

"We're not staying," Frank said innocently, lifting the muffin from Eamon's fingers and taking an enormous bite. "Just dropped by to take the kids on a little harbor cruise." Still chewing, he cadged a shrimp from the trio forming a Martha Stewart rosette at the plate's rim.

"Sorry," Elizabeth repeated during Mrs. Sykes's ensuing nonresponse. She did notice that the sisters had arranged for an especially large jar of jelly for her friends. It made her feel even guiltier for polluting the air. She tried to convince herself that her and her father's surprise slovenly appearance was not her fault.

Frank had driven the battered old truck directly from the dock to the bed-and-breakfast after he and his daughter had pulled their lobster traps and delivered the goods to market. Actually, the pair looked and smelled rather good, considering what they had spent their morning accomplishing. Mrs. Sykes, however, was unimpressed.

Her withering glance assured Elizabeth that she could have stopped her father if she had really *tried*.

"Would have showered up, Mrs. Sykes," Frank continued unapologetically, "but there's no point, since we're just headin' back out."

Elizabeth could feel unfamiliar eyes boring holes in the back of her flannel shirt. Martha smothered a giggle in her napkin. Mrs. Sykes did not deign to respond. She turned her back on Frank and served the breakfast plates to the waiting guests.

Miss Locke made her entrance to clear the finished tables, including Martha and Eamon's. Unlike her younger sister, she stopped in her tracks only briefly.

Martha was clearly enjoying herself, but Elizabeth could not help noticing that Eamon had the common decency to look embarrassed on the Wills' behalf.

"I am *so* sorry," Elizabeth repeated, backing her way to the foyer exit.

"Are you kidding?" Martha said to Elizabeth's retreating face. "We'd *love* a boat ride, wouldn't we, Eamon?" She rose from her place and pushed her chair under the table.

Eamon smiled wanly.

"Sure," he answered. "Sure. You mean, on the ocean?"

Frank clapped the younger man on the back.

"Would off'ah you mo'ah, but that's all she wrote when

you're headed east." Frank applied a liberal layer of jelly to the remaining piece of toast on Martha's bread plate, folded it in half, and finished it. Turning to the riveted diners, he saluted. "Would take you all, but don't have the room. Enjoy your stay!" Then, to the Robsons, he said, "Don't both'ah with sweat'ahs. Got extra gear on tha' boat."

" 'Bye, Mrs. Sykes. 'Bye, Miss Locke," Martha waved. "See you later." She took Eamon's hand and led him through the foyer and out the front door. Elizabeth had already escaped to the dubious sanctuary of Frank's pickup, wishing that Ginny were there to give her a cigarette.

She noticed Eamon hanging back behind Martha and Frank. He did not look like a happy puppy. Nonetheless, he helped his wife into the back of the truck at her insistence and settled himself into the front seat with Frank.

Elizabeth had wondered where they were going to sit. She should have known it would be in back, where the Labrador retriever and gun rack ought to travel.

"Is Eamon all right?" Elizabeth asked Martha. "He looks a little green around the gills."

"Oh, yes," Martha answered, settling onto the ridged flatbed, "he just gets seasick at the mention of the word 'sea.' I wouldn't miss this for the world."

"There's Dramamine somewhere on board."

"Good!" Martha shouted over the engine's complaints.

Elizabeth was thrown on top of her friend as Frank careered out onto the beach road. Through the rear window into the cab, she could see the white of Eamon's knuckles on the dashboard.

Eamon insisted on rowing the overloaded dory out to the *Curmudgeon II*'s mooring. Frank allowed it benevolently. Once aboard, Elizabeth forced a Dr Pepper and a seasickness pill on Eamon before she cast off. Martha scrambled onto the bow to raise the marine-radio antenna without having to be asked.

It was just like the old days, except that Elizabeth had the feeling that some poor innocent was going to end up barfing.

Frank was not completely insensitive. Not totally. When Eamon's wobbling threatened to spill Frank's beer, he offered to let the younger man steer.

"Keeping your eye on the horizon settles the stomach, ya know." He turned over the wheel. "Just don't plow down any of them buoys." Eamon looked panicked, but stayed silent, steering to save his soul. "Wouldn't want you t'have to go over the side to unfrig the screws." Eamon shook his head and stared straight ahead.

"What happened to the *Curmudgeon I?*" Martha shouted over the crank of the turbine. "I loved that boat. Remember skipping school and taking the guys out to the lighthouse?"

"I remember. Ginny ended up getting us home, and I was grounded for two weeks. As for the old *Curmudgeon,* don't ask," Elizabeth shouted back, working her way to the front of the boat. "I'll take over, Eamon. Just stand next to me and watch the horizon until the medicine kicks in." Frank grabbed two beers and joined Martha aft to enjoy the ride.

After some conservative female navigating, Eamon seemed to settle down and even tried sightseeing as Frank periodically pointed out one point of interest after another.

Elizabeth could not hear any of her friend's and father's conversation, but they were laughing and chugging beers and Dr Peppers like there was no tomorrow. On his trip back to the cooler to replenish, Frank pointed to the left.

"Might s'well dig us some clams whilst we're about it."

Elizabeth glanced over at Eamon. Since he seemed resigned to his fate, she decided not to get into a round-robin argument with her father. She would dig the damned clams and savor the prospect of an eventual knock-down, drag-out.

As they cruised past the state beach, Elizabeth could see the Fish and Game boys, as well as other uniforms, walking the sand and stooping to gather debris into bright yellow bags.

She knew she should have opened the gallery. With the beach taken away, the tourists would have to find some other way to spend their time and money.

Sun bunnies always seemed disoriented when their blankets got impounded for more than a day—by weather or by the government. She wished for the continuation of all such low attention spans.

Above all, she hoped to hell that Dick Dawley and the Pebble Beach entrepreneurs were not profiting when she could not. Fatalistically, she knew they were, though.

Fatalistic seemed to be the word of the day.

Eamon tossed the heavy three-pronged anchor off the side at the clam flats and did not complain in the slightest when informed that he was expected to jump over the side into the waist-deep water wearing his new Docksiders and then wade to the sandy hunting ground.

Frank secured the clam buckets and digging equipment to a lobster buoy and jumped from the lee.

"Damned gulls!" He wiped a drizzle of whitish gray excrement from the sample bumper sticker he had slapped onto the back of the boat.

Elizabeth helped lower Martha and Eamon into the freezing water, agreeing it was cold enough to kill a penguin.

She wanted to scream, herself, when she hit the surf, dragging the floating buckets behind, but she refused to give Frank the pleasure.

"Good," Frank pronounced, taking the beach like Iwo Jima, "we got the place to our own selves." He handed Martha a bucket and a clam rake: three curved steel fingers protruding from a palm-sized wood handle into which were burned the letters "E. Will." "Make yourself useful," he instructed, and threw the other bucket to Eamon.

Martha took over happily. "Just look for the little holes in the sand; that's where the clams are. Dig down with the rake and try not to crack too many shells." She demonstrated. "Try to get mostly clams that are bigger than the span between the prongs. Those are legal, but you can take up to twenty percent under size without getting busted."

"Don't we need a license or anything?" Eamon asked.

"Silly boy." Frank pulled another beer from his pants pocket.

"Yes," Elizabeth answered. Eamon looked guilty, although he still had not done anything even mildly larcenous. "Fish and Game are busy, and if they *should* show up, just hand your peck to Dad, and I'll grab Martha's. Strangely enough, Dad and I are both legal. I guess it doesn't matter who actually does the digging as long as we don't bag over the limit."

"And I'm real scrupulous about that," Frank said, and sat on the damp sand for a little upright nap. "Ethics R Us."

"Right," Elizabeth grumped.

Martha found a rich digging area and called Eamon over. Elizabeth doubted her friend was going to be able to wrangle herself a convert to the ways of the sea, but left the couple alone for a try.

She had a thundering headache, anyway. The last thing she wanted to do was hunker over a rake and pump more blood into her head, so she wandered aimlessly on the long, narrow sandbar.

A small swell of a dune at the farthest end sported what appeared to Elizabeth to be a stand of horsetail fern. The primitive plant actually fetched a good price at the university for first-year botany students to study. She tromped across the packed sand; since she was seeing MacKay that night, anyway, she figured she might as well make some money out of her afternoon off.

The minimal root systems pulled out easily, and Elizabeth had accumulated a healthy fistful of specimens by the time she worked her way over the crest of the dune and down toward the water. There was a pile of the common seaweed, laminaria, stinking to high heaven and crawling with green crabs at the ocean edge. Several sea gulls screamed their irritation at the invasion of their territory before taking to air in an explosion of flapping wings.

"Damned gulls," she spat, her heart thudding.

Elizabeth heard Eamon exclaim from beyond her sight. He sounded happy, though the wind carried his exact words out to sea. It pleased her, for some reason, and she turned her attention back to the lump of stinking weeds.

Laminaria often attached itself to mussels for ballast. Eamon might get a kick out of some handpicked mussels, too. Elizabeth took and held a deep breath to further explore whether or not there was any bounty to be had from the slimy mess. If there was, she would just brace for it, inhale the rotten odor, and suffer a little.

What the hell! She'd bring back a couple of crabs while she was at it. A friendship thing, she assured herself. No meat in them, to speak of, but what does a boy from northern Canada know, anyway? The stupid things make good lobster bait, if nothing else.

Laying the ferns to one side, Elizabeth knelt down. Crabs might make easy catching, but difficult holding. The pincers could take a good hunk out of even an experienced hand.

Spotting a likely captive, Elizabeth positioned herself to make a fast grab at its rear—and unarmed—end. Out of oxygen, she inhaled reluctantly and quietly. Noxious fumes forced her to mouth breathing. She could almost taste the odor. Slowly, she moved her fingers toward the feeding crustacean.

Whatever its meal, the crab was intent on having it; and Elizabeth was intent on having the crab. She cursed her own stubbornness.

After all, what was the point? It was not as if there were not thousands of crabs available for show and tell, whose capture would not make her sick to her stomach. She decided to give it one snatch and, whether success or failure, get on with her life. Just one try.

With dogged concentration, Elizabeth focused on the backside of the animal, tensed, and sprang.

The crab whizzed sideways and into the tangle of vegetation, leaving Elizabeth with nothing but a handful of wet, mushy . . .

She screamed and fell backward.

. . . face.

FIVE

EAMON ROBSON MAY have been an inlander, but he knew the difference between the shriek of dislocated waterfowl and the reflexive wail of human terror.

"Just gulls," Martha assured her husband as the scream cut the air. Frank did not seem to rouse from his nap, though he did, in fact, open one eye and watch three extremely annoyed sea gulls dart and soar at the far side of the sand bar.

Eamon dropped his half-full peck of small native clams and tore across the packed sand at full rugby speed. His Docksiders were sodden, the bottoms of his feet sliding every which way in the slippery linings. He kicked off the impediments midstride and hurled himself over the thatch of horsetail fern in the direction of the screech.

Elizabeth sat on her heels, her body arched backward and braced at a seemingly impossible angle by rigid arms thrust behind her in the grainy dune. Eamon slid down the incline, dragging to a stop just behind her, and grasped her shoulders firmly in his hands.

The muscles in Elizabeth's back were flexed hard and immovable as a granite jetty; Eamon could not turn Elizabeth to face him without breaking a bone. He crawled on aching knees around to face her.

What he saw did not reassure him. Elizabeth's mouth hung slack, her breathing a slow, dogged pant. Eamon quickly checked her as well as he could without risking any further injury, but found no cuts, bruises, bleeding—nothing.

"Elizabeth?" Eamon whispered, afraid of frightening her even more than she obviously had been. "Elizabeth?" he repeated, a bit louder, very much afraid she was experiencing some kind of seizure, out in the middle of nowhere. The slow panting continued.

Frank would know.

Eamon scuttled back to the top of the dune and shouted over the bird screams and ocean sounds.

"FRANK! Martha. *Over here, now!"*

Eamon felt an iron slap to his ankle. He whipped around to find Elizabeth trying to get his attention. Her lips were closed, and the panting was more controlled.

"I'm okay," she said, her voice gravelly but calm enough. "I'm okay. Just give me a minute." She blew a deep breath through pursed lips. "I have to get back to the *Curmudgeon.*"

Frank and Martha arrived at a run, stopping so short at the top of the pile that their feet sent a shower of sand into Eamon's and Elizabeth's hair.

"What's the matter?" Martha asked. Her amber eyes were wide in her oval face. Instinctively, she worked down the descent and put an arm around Elizabeth. "Biz, what's the matter? Are you hurt?"

"Shee-ut!" Frank said in a low voice from above them all. The big man planted one foot in front of the other and, in deliberate strides, came toward the others. And past them.

Frank Will stood at the edge of the water, back to his daughter.

"Shee-ut," he repeated to himself.

"Frank," Eamon shouted, "I think Elizabeth is having some kind of seizure. For God's sake, will you get over here and help?"

"I'm all right," Elizabeth said for what felt to her the hundredth time. Frank bent and pulled a clump of seaweed from near his feet and flung it into the water.

"Hell of a lot bett'ah than Est'ah Williams, he'ah."

The bloated face of what had once been a pretty young woman looked skyward from her bridal bed of laminaria. Crabs scattered like roaches from the exposed area.

Eamon Robson leaned politely to one side and vomited the remains of his lovely Wild Rose breakfast.

Elizabeth insisted on wading back out to the lobster boat to call Ginny and the Coast Guard by marine radio to meet them at the clam flats. She was not being noble, she needed the shockingly frigid water against her thighs and belly to jolt her back into some sort of normalcy.

It was not enough.

After notifying the authorities, she dove headlong into the deep water and paddled her way back to the group waiting with the body. Once on land, she stripped off her sodden flannel shirt and allowed the cool breeze to dry her skin. Her T-shirt was stiff with salt by the time Ginny arrived on the scene.

The police skiff was shallow enough abeam for Ginny to plow directly onto the sandbar. By stepping gingerly from the bow, the chief did not even dampen her shoes.

Frank waved his position from the dune. Ginny observed her best friend's bedraggled condition without comment, and handed Elizabeth a pack of cigarettes and lighter from her uniform breast pocket.

"Thanks."

"You know, Biz," Ginny commented, "I think it's time you started smoking." The two women walked toward the others.

"You mean buying my own?" Elizabeth lit up and inhaled to her ankles.

"I mean, you really need something else to keep your hands busy."

Frank and Eamon stood under the canopy of the *Curmudgeon,* drinking beer during the entire trip back to the mooring. Frank continued to indicate interesting features of the area, more to keep himself busy than for Eamon's edification.

Seasickness forgotten, Eamon nodded politely and popped fresh brews when it was expected. Every so often, he turned around to make sure that his wife and Elizabeth were doing all right at the aft of the boat.

Elizabeth chain-smoked the entire pack of Camels, being careful to exhale away from Martha, who was not looking in peak condition, herself. Martha wanted private time, but once she had it, she was not feeling particularly chatty. The two women sat, side by side on the peeling slats, examining each other surreptitiously.

After fourteen years apart, neither had changed very much. Both were still thin and pretty: Martha Ann in her ethereally cool, chiseled fashion; Elizabeth in her no-nonsense, hearty, and freckled way. All the girls from Dovekey tended toward the tall side, from Avis at the low end to Ginny at the top.

WASPy, Elizabeth thought. All of us. If a random citizen of Beijing were shown a class photo, he probably would not be able to tell one of us from another. "Homogenized" came to her mind, and then various synonyms.

Dovekey Beach was not the kind of community that expected a lot of variety among its residents. Usually the only thing that kept things interesting at all was the annoying influx of strangers. Short ones, ethnic ones, rude ones, rich ones. Dead ones.

This season was shaping up as more than merely interesting. Elizabeth searched her mind for the proper descriptive word.

Macabre.

She knew there was a first time for everything, but there was something seriously wrong with having all the firsts come at the *same* time. Even putting her incipient cynicism aside, something was rotten in Dovekey.

Worse than that, two people she cared about very much had scheduled themselves right into the middle of it. Ginny was busier than a one-armed paperhanger, and could not be everywhere at once.

Elizabeth made up her mind that wherever Ginny was not, she could be. That would mean an extra trip after the *Curmudgeon II* tied up, before she cleaned up and had her private hysterics.

First things first. And friends and family always came at the top of the list. Elizabeth realized how silent Martha Robson had become.

"So," she began feebly. "What's it like living in Canada?"

"Clean," Martha answered, knowing it was the answer Elizabeth expected. In fairness, she elaborated. "Like America on Prozac, I guess. It's almost like living in the States, but"—she thought for a moment—"a little like breaking in a new pair of shoes. They look good. You like them. You know that eventually they'll be as comfortable as the grungy ones you ought to throw away, but can't."

"How long did it take?"

"I don't know yet. I'm still a U.S. citizen."

"You're kidding," Elizabeth said, chauvinistically pleased, but still surprised. "Your folks, too?"

Martha lifted the sweat-soaked hair from the back of her neck and angled her perfect face toward the sun. "I really don't know," she answered after a pause. "After Eamon and I married, they moved again to somewhere in Vancouver and started themselves a second family."

"Oh, you're lying!" Elizabeth poked Martha in the side. "Bert and Sarah? Nahhh." She looked at Martha for a denial or a "gotcha!" Martha simply kept her eyes on the horizon, her face a mask of boredom with the subject.

"So how come you're still living with your father and not married?"

"Smooth, Marty. If you want to change the subject, all you have to do is ask." She took Martha's hand in hers and smoked with her left. Wonders truly never ceased. Despite the peculiarity that both women had ended up functionally motherless, it did not present as the best of times to pry into what appeared to be a still-raw abandonment issue. Elizabeth searched for a passive topic. "Poor Eamon looks crummy."

"Doesn't he just. Poor baby!"

"Maybe we should have Doc Ryan give him a look-see."

"Doc Ryan is still practicing? Wow." Martha released her hand from Elizabeth's. "I, well, I just assumed he'd be retired by now. Isn't that amazing."

"He says he's going to keep practicing until he gets it right." Elizabeth watched Martha's face for any sign of the genuine astonishment she had voiced, but there was none. She was as implacable as she had always been.

Elizabeth would have given a lot for that kind of composure, but she knew the genetic dice were loaded against her and accepted it.

"That sounds like Dr. Ryan."

"You know, Doc would love to see you," she prodded for Eamon's sake.

70

"I think between Miss Locke, Mrs. Sykes, and me, we can take care of Eamon all right. He'll be fine."

"We'll just take a rain check on dinner tonight," Elizabeth offered. Neither Eamon nor Martha looked to her as though they would just bounce back from their morning's adventure.

"I don't see why," Martha answered. "Sitting around and thinking about ancient history can make you crazy."

"Finding two bodies in the last two days may be history, but it isn't exactly ancient."

"Whatever." Martha opened her eyes. "It'll be fun. Just like the old days."

Except, Elizabeth thought, completely different.

The skin of the body was tattered and shredded in patches, but, aside from the superficial ravaging by scavengers, at least the corpse was fundamentally intact.

It was difficult for Dr. Ben Ryan to be grateful for anything that evening. He was not having a lucky tourist season. Stupid, really. After the logistic difficulties following Al Jenness's murder earlier in the year, it was his own foolishness that had made him agree to act as Dovekey Beach coroner. One thousand dollars a year.

Ben Ryan figured that he ended up signing the death certificates in the area, anyway. People in the village seemed to live about forever. Doctor Ryan, himself, was a chain-smoking, inactive man in his mid-seventies.

How was he supposed to know that, almost the minute he agreed to his thankless moonlighting job, total strangers would start coming to town for, what seemed to be, the sole purpose of dropping dead? And, unlike the locals, the tourists showed— to Ryan's mind—an unnatural interest in the precise cause of their loved ones' deaths.

The doctor harrumphed to himself and flipped on the fluorescent light overhead. Three dead tourists in one week. Talk about bad luck. He would not be investing in the Tri-State Megabuck lottery this week.

Of course, neither would the three tourists.

Doc Ryan pulled a scalpel from the black leather folding case at the corpse's head. There were the pathetic remains of sprays of baby's breath twined in the dark hair.

A little something for the mortician to deal with.

The condemned moved lethargically in the bubbling water as chatting couples passed by in disinterest. Wrecked traps and torn netting hung everywhere, enlivened by a sporadic knot of special note or colored glass ball for which no one knew the purpose.

"Quaint?" MacKay asked. "Flankers don't use the word 'quaint.'"

"Tell it to Eamon Robson," Elizabeth said to her date. She looked around the restaurant for their party, and almost walked into the saltwater tank that displayed the "choose-your-own-dinner" lobsters. She wondered how rank amateurs would ever be able to tell if they were eating their chosen victim, or a pre-prepared ringer. "I still can't believe he and Martha are up to this. I don't mind telling you, it wasn't my favorite day this year."

"Eamon's a damned good wing forward."

"I thought he was a flanker."

"Same thing."

"Then why can't you call it the same thing?" Men, Elizabeth grumped silently. She felt lousy, but went to a lot of trouble to look good. Mostly to punish MacKay for never taking her out on a Saturday night.

"You look terrific, by the way."

MacKay was an undeclared sucker for Elizabeth's legs and

was very much enjoying the way she looked in her new teal minidress. But he had learned the hard way not to be specific in his compliments. He had once mentioned how much he liked her hair long, and the next day she had clipped herself nearly bald. Perverse—but then, so was he.

"Thanks. Can you see . . . oh, God!" Elizabeth slumped, which was very unlike her. "Dad invited Claire Wallis to join us. I don't believe it."

"In my opinion, I think your father's dating is uncharacteristically healthy."

Elizabeth gave MacKay a look that would flash-freeze a bluefin tuna.

"My father does not date."

"Right."

"This is Monday night. *Saturday* is date night," Elizabeth explained, a bit emphatically if one had asked Charles MacKay, Ph.D.

Claire Wallis was a vision in mint green, shoes and bag to match, and she was hanging on Frank Will's arm like Spanish moss. At least, Elizabeth thought so. No one else appeared thoroughly disgusted. MacKay pulled the strawberry blonde to the table without straining himself overmuch.

Claire was willing to go the extra mile.

"Elizabeth! Frank was just telling me what an awful day you've had. I am *so* sorry. Are you all right? Is there anything I can do to help?"

You could go home, Elizabeth thought. *You could do your volunteer work in Zimbabwe.*

"I'm fine, Claire."

"You don't look fine, dear," Claire said, "and you know how much time I've spent as a candy striper over the years. I'm almost a professional."

As long as you give it away, Claire, Elizabeth mused, *You will never attain professional status.*

MacKay sensed danger and interjected.

"Have you seen the blue lobster, Claire?" he asked.

"Why, yes, Charles," she fluttered, "but not with a marine biologist."

Botanist, you slut! Elizabeth corrected silently.

"I'd like a closer look," MacKay lied, and led Claire out of the death-by-verbal-abuse zone back to the lobster tank. En route, they ran into Martha and Eamon on the way to the table. MacKay was relieved to be getting reinforcements, Elizabeth noticed contemptuously.

She thought it was swishy of him and then, despite herself, admitted she was not in the best mood ever for a romantic evening or personality analysis. She promised herself to try and behave, or, at least, repress the more antisocial of her inclinations.

Her self-imposed pep talk included the fact that she had a date (even though it was not, technically, date night), she would finally have a chance to really talk to Martha, and that it was not her body being autopsied at Doc Ryan's. Her line of thought was not totally sunny, but it was the best Elizabeth could do under the circumstances.

And it looked as though it was better than Martha Robson could do. From twenty feet away, Elizabeth could see that there was something wrong. Martha had pulled herself perfectly erect, and lowered her jaw to look at Claire Wallis from through her upper eyelashes. It was a nearly perfect imitation of a pose from Princess Diana's days as "Shy Di," but Martha Ann's habit dated back much farther than that, and Elizabeth remembered it well.

Claire Wallis lived on Whipple Road, right next door to the big old farmhouse where Martha had grown up. Elizabeth could not wait to pump Martha for Claire's dirty little secrets.

To her disappointment, Elizabeth watched Martha peck

Claire on the cheek and take her hand. Pleasant introductions were made, and the newly formed alliance joined Elizabeth and her father.

"Well," Claire gushed to Frank, "don't I just feel twenty years younger! Why, it seems like just yesterday that I was watching our little Martha Ann out in the yard."

Martha blushed furiously.

"We actually *were* shorter, once," Elizabeth assured Eamon.

"You know," Claire plunged ahead, "you girls ought to attend our next DAR meeting. Once initiated, your membership is for life. And it would be such *fun* to have the two of you back in the fold."

"When is the meeting?" Martha asked, looking for all the world as though she were really interested.

"Next Wednesday. We're going to be discussing the importance of New Hampshire's vote, ratifying the Constitution."

"Really?" Eamon inquired.

"Really," Martha confirmed.

"I should have studied up before we made this trip," he said, looking around. "This place is terrific," Eamon beamed with pride over his choice of dining establishments. There was not a local face in the room outside the Will reservation, but he could not have known that. "I'll bet the lobster is great here."

Everyone at the table knew that lobster is pretty much lobster wherever it gets boiled, but no one said it. Claire cocked her head provocatively at Frank and took Eamon's arm.

"Let's just go over and pick out your favorite, then, shall we, Eamon?" she asked, leading him away. Elizabeth could hear the final dregs of Claire's soliloquy. "I like to name them before they go to the kitchen. It makes it so much more personal, don't you think? I think yours should be called Diefenbaker, after my favorite Canadian Prime Minister."

"Well, that's an incentive," Frank commented.

"I'm going to be sick," Elizabeth threatened. "Martha, come to the ladies' room with me." She dragged her friend on a quick detour by the cigarette machine, pumped in every quarter they both had to get a pack of something menthol, and then settled herself on the lavatory counter for a quick smoke and all the dirt Martha could come up with.

"I don't know what you're talking about," Martha said. "I haven't thought about Claire Wallis in fourteen years."

"Oh, come on," Elizabeth urged, "I saw the look on your face when you saw her. Now, spill your guts."

Martha brushed her hair, put on some lipstick, and then washed her hands.

"She and her husband were not close friends of my parents. We lived next door to each other for about three years, but I didn't know anything about them."

"Liar!"

"Really. Mr. Wallis was a selectman, and Mrs. Wallis was a do-gooder. You know more about them than I do."

"Her. *He's* dead. Probably his preference."

"Biz, for heaven's sake," Martha said, smoothing down one of Elizabeth's errant curls. "Funny, though, in a sick way. When did he die?"

"Five years ago, this month. Why is it funny? He was always the nice one." Elizabeth was really hoping Martha had some inside information on rampant husband beating at the Wallis home.

"Oh, nothing, really. Mrs. Wallis just always told him that if tourist season didn't kill him, nothing would. And maybe it finally did."

"Any physically violent fights? Maybe late-night visitors when Mr. Wallis was out of town?" Elizabeth was desperate.

"Nothing!" Martha pulled the cigarette from between Elizabeth's fingers and ran it under the faucet. "Now, let's get back to dinner. I'm worried about Eamon. He hasn't been feeling very well, and that rugby game the other day has caught up with him. He's walking like a hundred-year-old woman."

"Why are you lying to me?" Elizabeth asked. It was a sincere query, her hatred of Claire as secondary as it could ever be.

Martha opened the powder-room door for her friend and waited for her to go through.

"You must be insane to start smoking again."

Elizabeth gave up the battle, if not the war.

"I told you, Martha, if you want to change the subject, just ask."

Appetizers were already served when the women got back to their party. Eamon stood and pulled out chairs for both Martha and Elizabeth. Frank and MacKay were busy serving themselves from a plate of stuffed clams.

"Frank went ahead and ordered for all of us," Claire said, adoration in her eyes.

"Except me," Eamon said.

"Damned fool ordered lobster," Frank told his daughter. "Just had it last night, and you know what 'priced according to market' means. Mary on a bicycle. The Canadian dollar isn't that strong, boy."

"This is an occasion." Eamon approved a blush Zinfandel bottled in special lobster-molded glass. "I'd like to propose a toast." The waitress poured a half-glass of the pink wine for everyone at the table. "To my beautiful wife, Martha Ann Drake Robson; thank you for sharing your life with me."

"That was beautiful, Eamon," Claire gushed. "I guess it's tragedies like the one you witnessed this afternoon that makes one grateful for all of God's gifts."

Elizabeth repressed her brains out.

Dinner arrived, and despite Frank's criticisms of Eamon's choice, he snapped the spinnerettes off the lobster and sucked every one down to the shell. Claire obviously disapproved, but Frank was incapable of shame.

"Waste not, want not."

"Thank you, Benjamin Franklin," Elizabeth said before MacKay and Eamon launched into what would be a dinner-long discussion of the fine points of union versus league rugby. With the exception of Claire, the women were too tired to institute their own conversation or participate in the men's.

Frank just enjoyed dinner out in a restaurant—even if it was a tourist trap.

Elizabeth lapsed into a masochistic pondering of whether or not Claire was going to be in the house by the time she and MacKay got home. Exhausted, she could barely work up the mandatory shudder of revulsion.

Martha was as lost in thought as she, and Elizabeth realized she no longer had any idea what sort of thoughts those might be. Fourteen years can be the blink of eye, or a very, very long time.

Eamon paid the bill and did not notice when Frank slipped an extra ten-dollar tip under his plate. Elizabeth saw the move and put the money she had ready back in her oversized canvas pocketbook. Their reputation among the restaurant personnel of Dovekey was secure.

Frank Will did not give a rat's ass what the locals thought of him generally, as long as they did not think he was cheap, specifically.

That would be vulgar, as opposed to acceptably eccentric. The Will family had ethics, if not a clear home advantage on the well-balanced playing field.

At the door, Frank finalized the niceties.

"Thanks, Eamon," he said, patting the mound of stomach beneath his Sunday-go-to-meeting flannel shirt. "I'm full as a tick."

Claire clearly disapproved of his descriptive choice, but slid her arm through Frank's for the walk to the parking lot.

And separate cars, Elizabeth hoped. MacKay had picked her up at the gallery, so she did not know for a fact, and she cursed herself for the oversight.

"Our pleasure," came the reply. Eamon wrapped his arm around Martha's waist at the door; Elizabeth and MacKay walked side by side with the other couple to the Robsons' green Taurus.

The Lobster Haven hostess commented to the cashier how beautiful the foursome was in the moonlight: the men so tall and, she could not help notice, well-built; both women so lovely in such different ways. And good tippers, the waitress interjected.

Surprising, for Canucks, they all agreed.

"Hey, Eamon," MacKay said as Eamon settled his wife in the front seat of their car. "We have a game next Saturday against Beacon Hill, and we could use some of your speed. What do you say?"

"Sounds great, if I'm still walking. I don't mind telling you I'm feeling pretty beat up from the last game. I didn't know I had so many muscles to pull." Eamon closed Martha's door and came around to the driver's side.

"That's because you were wearing cleats the wrong size," MacKay diagnosed, looking at the other man's feet. "Twelve?" Eamon nodded. "I have a spare pair of boots I can loan you."

"Done," Eamon shook MacKay's paw. "Where and when?"

"Saturday on the common. 'A' side plays at noon, 'B' at two. Keg on the pitch, and we host a party at Rosa's after."

"See you, then," Eamon agreed, looking perkier than he had for the last two hours.

MacKay and Elizabeth watched the car pull away, Martha

79

pointing the direction in the glow of the dashboard lighting. To Elizabeth's surprise, MacKay took her hand in his and led her on foot toward the town beach across the street.

"Nice night for a walk," MacKay explained, sitting on the waist-high granite wall and kicking off his shoes. Elizabeth hoisted herself up next to him and did the same. "So you're a Daughter of the American Revolution, huh?"

"Well, it was really Martha's idea. She was the gung-ho one, and kind of dragged Ginny and me along for the ride."

"Ginny, too? Will wonders never cease."

"Well, they did cease. When Martha left, Ginny and I never went back to another meeting. Our side won. End of story."

"Aren't you the patriotic one, though," MacKay said, and flicked his sock at Elizabeth's cheek.

"You're the one who's trying to kill the Commonwealth." She swung her legs toward the water and dropped to the sand.

"Who?" MacKay asked, all innocence and big bare feet.

"Who?" Elizabeth mimicked. "Eamon. Our neighbor to the north."

MacKay took both pairs of shoes and set them side by side on the wall before, once again, taking Elizabeth's hand in his.

"Oh, be a man, woman. He's just a little cleated up." They walked to the low tide water's edge, twenty yards east. The lights from the ecology center MacKay supervised blinked from seven miles offshore.

"Yeah, I heard that." Elizabeth dug her toes into the heavy sand and propelled a lump into the water. "But, man to man, he looks like forty miles of trampled bear shit."

"Nice talk," MacKay reprimanded, pulling her toward him for a kiss in a sweep from the Whaleback Lighthouse. "Eamon's as strong as an ox. Better than that, he's fast. He could run the piss out of that little Cornell flanker we've had to play."

"I don't know." Elizabeth ran her hands around MacKay's

waist and clutched the material at his back. "He's been looking kind of puny to me, the last couple of days."

MacKay kissed Elizabeth again.

"Yeah, well, it's been a helluva couple of days."

She kissed him back, forgetting the Robsons for the moment and getting into it, despite the logistics.

"Have you ever thought of getting an apartment on the mainland?" she asked.

"You ever thought of moving out of your father's house?" They moved back onto dry sand and prepared to sit.

Elizabeth balked. "Damn, I forgot," she said. "There's been stuff washing up on the beach."

"Don't I know it," MacKay tried to pull Elizabeth down beside him. "The biohazard boys have been all over my ass like eczema. We were the first group they suspected, the fascists. Anyway, we don't stock most of the lab waste they turned up." He tugged on Elizabeth's arm. "Besides, this beach is dead clean. They only got junk off the state beach." Elizabeth relented and fell to her knees next to MacKay.

"Wait a minute," Elizabeth thought aloud, running her fingers through the surface of the beach. "We didn't see anything on the clam flats, either."

"That's not entirely true," MacKay commented sourly. "Unless you've gotten used to tripping over washed-up drowning victims."

"Hardly. But that's my point. Don't you think it's strange?"

"Damned strange, even for Dovekey Beach. You may not believe this, but I have never actually discovered a corpse in my whole, long, lurid life." He reached for Elizabeth, who pulled away. The moonlight was so bright that she could almost make out the green of his eyes.

"I mean," she directed his hand away from her cheek,

"*where* things are washing up. The state beach is no more than a mile north of here, and the clam flats another mile north of that."

"And?"

"And, that woman I found was last seen alive at the state beach. We can assume she drowned there and was taken by the current to get caught up on the clam flats."

"Yes, we could assume that, but both of us *know* the current runs in that direction."

"Exactly." Elizabeth rested her case. Prematurely, judging by MacKay's reaction.

"Have you ever made love on the beach?" he asked.

Elizabeth ignored the question.

"The current runs straight south to north along this part of the coast. The ocean isn't that fastidious about where it spills its guts. There should have been some—a little—garbage dropped off here, too, on its way to the state beach."

"Not necessarily."

"All right," Elizabeth conceded so quickly, MacKay knew she had more ammunition to fire, "but even if—for no logical reason—this beach is as clean as a dog's mouth, something besides that poor dead woman should have shown up at the flats. Wouldn't you think, if the body was all tangled in the seaweed, there should have been a piece of trash, too? Unless . . . "

"What?"

"The medical waste was never *in* the water. As if it was all just purposely dumped on the state beach. Why would anyone do that?"

MacKay realized his romance time was being cut short, and possibly out entirely.

"I guess you have no idea what it costs to properly dispose of hazardous medical materials. It's an unconscionable percentage of The Eternal Sea Group's budget, and we do no work at all with human biology. Our marine bacteriological adjunct is about three percent of our research."

Elizabeth dug into her canvas handbag, and pulled out a gallon-size plastic bag, stuffed with what appeared to be quilt batting. She handed it to MacKay.

"Could you make it five percent for July?"

MacKay held the transparent bag up to the moonlight, and made out the outline of two syringes bundled up in various lengths of bandaging material.

"You have been stealing evidence in a federal investigation."

"You could put it that way. This was caught up in the rocks off to the side of the beach. The next tide would have taken it off, probably." MacKay looked at her dubiously. She dug in. "A child might have stepped on it."

"Sure."

"You'll have your people analyze the samples, then?"

"I'll have my grad students look at them, when they have the time, which they shouldn't. Liz, why don't you let the feds do what they do?"

"Because they take too long to do it, and do it badly." She pursed her lips. Subject: closed.

MacKay rose and held out his free hand to Elizabeth.

"A true New Hampshireman's response, if I ever heard one." He pulled her to her feet, the mood gone. "You all will be the death of me, yet."

The abdomen was laid open from breast to bowel, face covered with one of Edith Ryan's special cross-stitched dish towels. The lungs lay heaped in the aluminum scale Ben Ryan had been using off and on (mostly off) for thirty years. He adjusted his reading glasses and squinted at the numbers. Then he took off the glasses and squinted at the indicator again.

"Must be wrong," he muttered to himself, though he did

83

not truly believe it. He examined the pasty gray throat for signs of bruising or abrasion, and found none.

The doctor wiped his bloody scalpel on another of Edith's fancy handiwork and sliced a neat line down the throat of the deceased.

He hoped his stitching was still as good as his wife's. He had just made the kind of incision that no mortician could hide in a hairline or under clothing. But, then, no body could be prettied up after two days in the water, anyway. Ryan adjusted the cobra angle light down for a closer look at the exposed trachea.

Wearily, the old man reached to the tape recorder perched on the wheeled white enamel table to his left, and pressed Record before speaking aloud.

"Trachea closed up tighter than a virgin's thighs." His stomach growled and he checked his watch. "No water found in lungs. No trauma to throat area. Cause of death: suffocation. Natural causes: anaphylactic shock. Stomach contents minimal except for one-quarter to half inch undigested pieces of what appears to be lobster or other seafood. Probable profound allergic reaction."

Ben Ryan hit the Off button on the recorder and snapped off his latex gloves.

Before bagging the stomach contents for lab analysis, he thought he might as well get a bite to eat.

If this was going to be another red-tide poisoning year, the old man wanted to face it on a full belly.

SIX

Six-thirty in the morning seemed earlier than usual to Elizabeth. Perhaps, she considered, it was having to listen to Claire Wallis giggling in her mother's living room until 2:00 A.M. that had contributed to her advanced stage of sleep deprivation.

Perhaps the fact that her father had not personally hauled a trap out of the water for the entire morning had something to do with her irritability.

Frank steered the *Curmudgeon* through the maze of lobster buoys on their run back to shore, pretending he had not yet noticed that his elder daughter was not speaking to him, when, in fact, it was driving him crazy.

Elizabeth used the hook at the end of the six-foot pole like a weapon instead of a tool to catch the lines that ran from lobster pot to marker buoy. She hacked at the ropes as though they were snakes.

They unloaded their haul at the commercial dock without exchanging a word. Eager to force Elizabeth's hand, Frank hung out with the other men and let her do the heavy lifting. She was resolute.

As soon as their cargo was weighed and sorted, Frank offered to help: a ploy that had never failed to send his daughter into a tirade. Until that morning.

Desperate, Frank inquired during the truck ride back to the gallery, how business was. Elizabeth recognized a last-ditch effort when she heard one, and wordlessly ground the old Chevy's gears into first before turning off the ignition and marching directly into the shower on the second floor of the house.

When she came downstairs, dressed in a powder pink full-length dress and matching sandals, Frank had breakfast ready. Three eggs and five rashers of bacon apiece, including Petunia, who stood paws up on the table ready for the go ahead. Elizabeth ignored the cocker spaniel, too, but sat down to quickly eat her breakfast. She knew that if she said a word, every bit of spleen would pour out in a torrent and Frank would have won.

Not a chance.

Petunia, in her brain-dead fashion, was so agitated by the uncommonly fine-tuned household tension, that she trotted behind Elizabeth down the long drive to open the gallery. Feigning indifference, Frank followed the black furball down the hill.

He knew that if he started converting discarded lobster traps into tacky coffee tables while Elizabeth tried to paint or sell, it would drive her over the edge.

There were people in Dovekey Beach who would have commented, "That's not a drive, it's a short walk." Fortunately, none of them were present.

Elizabeth kept her back turned to both her father and his spoiled-rotten dog as she maneuvered the key in the old lock cylinder. Frank plucked a note handwritten on the back of a parking-violation ticket off the door window and handed it to Elizabeth. When she refused to acknowledge him, he tore noisily at the tape that had affixed it to the window.

She left her keys dangling in the door, grabbed the paper from his hand, glanced down, and read the scrawl twice.

"Oh, my God, no!"

Dick Dawley sat at the head of the long conference table. He was wearing a pale blue seersucker suit that looked as if it had been lifted from the costume department of *Jaws*. The two women and five men chowed down on danishes, oblivious.

"Okay," Dawley said, "so we agree to leave apprehension of that rat-bastard carnival to the state police."

Leo Bisset washed a mouthful of pastry down with luke-warm coffee before adding his two-cents-worth.

"Just like it's more than five miles either direction to get the hell *out* of state."

Dawley scowled, "So just what d'you want me to do, Leo?"

Eleanor Perkins came to the mayor's defense, in her own way.

"I'd say you've done about enough, Dick." Eleanor was uncomfortable leaving Ellie's Deli in the hands of a couple of high-school students for the entire morning and wanted to get back to work. "I move to close this meeting of the Pebble Beach Chamber of Commerce before tourist season is over and we're up to our butts in snow."

"Ayes" were heard all around.

"Now, wait a minute," Dawley held up his hand. "I think we have a situation evolvin' he'ah that can be turned to our advantage." Eleanor remained standing, but the others sat back down dutifully. The thieving carnival had put a damper on the enthusiasm of the tourist population for flashing cash. "Any of you been followin' the papers?" He held up a copy of that morning's *Dovekey Call* and waved it under Eleanor's nose. She swiped the lightweight weekly from his hand. "I have highlighted appropriate entries from all the local papers over the last three days."

Eleanor glanced at the front page.

"Two fat people in stupid costumes, so?" She tossed the paper to the table. Dick handed it back to her.

"Read," he instructed. She made a noise of disgust before beginning.

"Local heroes, Asa and Margaret Fleck, on the scene." Eleanor looked back up at Dawley. "So?"

"Keep reading," he pointed at the yellow paragraph beneath. She read to herself, and dropped the paper again.

"So, there was a kitchen fire at Vinnie's."

"Keep reading, for cry'in out loud."

The chamber of commerce leaned toward Eleanor as one. As soon as she finished one highlighted section, Dawley handed her another. And then another.

"Wow!" she breathed.

"What?" Leo asked.

"The tourists," Eleanor said. "They're droppin' like flies right over the town line."

"Talk about good luck!" Dick Dawley enthused.

Frank shut Petunia up in the Cape Cod kitchen and, for a change, insisted on driving the truck for himself. The good news was that Elizabeth was too upset to fear for her own life at the hands of Big Frank Will's creative driving skills.

Elizabeth was out of the cab before her father had brought the rattling rust bucket to a full stop, straddling two parking spaces. She narrowly avoided being struck by a Mercedes with M.D. plates rounding the circular drive, and bounded up the concrete ramp to the emergency room.

Dr. Ryan was signing papers at the triage desk. He handed

them to the nurse as Elizabeth came up beside him. She nodded to him, but addressed the nurse.

"You have a patient in intensive care?"

"Your name?" The nurse asked.

"Elizabeth Will," Dr. Ryan answered for her. "I'll take her in, Frannie."

"How bad is it?" Elizabeth asked.

"Pretty bad, I'm afraid," Doc answered and took her by the arm around a corner, following a red line painted onto the linoleum floor. "Convulsive seizure. We're running some tests, but"—Frank caught up with the pair—"we don't know anything, yet. Frank. Glad you're here." The three continued walking until they reached a heavy oak door, glassed from waist-level up. Behind the door, machinery hummed and flickered. "I hear you all had dinner together last night."

"Ayuh."

Elizabeth pressed both palms to the glass and peered in. The body in the bed was all but unrecognizable beneath its shroud of tubes, wires, and tape. Another nurse adjusted intravenous lines. Martha Robson sat like a statue at her husband's bedside, politely out of the way. Elizabeth could not attract her attention. Doc Ryan's questioning droned on. After some moments, she focused on one.

"So Eamon was the only one who had something different for dinner?" Ryan asked.

"Ayuh," Frank answered. "Lobster. Damned fool!"

"And no one else has complained of illness?"

"No," Elizabeth answered.

"Well, *could* be a lobster allergy," Ryan reasoned as he made a note in Eamon Robson's chart, "but it's a pretty severe reaction. Two in one week would be damned unusual."

"Two?" Frank asked. "That tourist woman's husband said

she knew she was allergic. Can't figure out why she risked it."

"That's not it. We had lobster the night before, too," Elizabeth said. "No allergic reaction at all. Unless the lobster was bad, I don't understand it." She waved again to Martha, who continued to stare at her husband. "And he picked out his own lobster at Lobster Haven, so it must have been alive. Selling dead ones is illegal."

"Eatin' one's suicidal," Frank added.

"And they're right out to see at Lobster Haven. Eamon and Claire went off especially to choose. I remember particularly," Elizabeth said, "because Claire was doing some weird thing about naming the lobsters before killing them. Sick. Even *I* would have trouble digesting something I knew on a first-name basis."

"This isn't indigestion, Liz," the doctor pointed out. "Eamon might have had the bad luck to pick himself out a tainted one, though. It happens."

Elizabeth knew that it did. But *so* rarely. Then she remembered the scene at the restaurant the night before.

"Dad had some, too," she said.

"No, suh," Frank denied. "Had the Fisherman's Platter, twelve-ninety-five, just like everybody else."

"Except," Elizabeth disagreed, "you cleaned out the spinnerettes. How do you feel?"

"You been with me all mornin'. I'm right as rain." The doctor looked closely at Frank's face. Frank pulled back. "Righter. Listen, Doc, I've had seafood poisonin' befo'ah. Ain't got it now."

"Well, I guess you'd know, Frank." Ryan looked almost disappointed.

"Wait a minute," Elizabeth interrupted. "Eamon was drafted into a game of rugby the morning he arrived. It looked pretty physical to me. Is it possible that Eamon got kicked in the head or something?"

"Rugby, huh?" Ryan considered. "I'd say a kick in the head would be probable. Thanks, Elizabeth. I'll order up an MRI and take a look-see."

There was a crash from behind the ICU door. Martha was pressed backward against the wall; the nurse shouted for Dr. Ryan.

Eamon Robson was convulsing.

Rose Sykes stood at the bow of the eighty-foot sightseeing vessel, public-address system in hand. The standing-room-only crowd hung on her every word. Mostly.

There were a few among the ticket holders simply trying to hold onto their lunches. The soft, low swells of the water were harder on those prone to seasickness than a high sea. A few other guests stared longingly toward the closed state beach, bitterly concerned about getting a truck-driver tan instead of something more befitting a holiday trip.

"A mile off to your right is the university's Piscatawk Island Ecology Center run in conjunction with The Eternal Sea Group. It is the largest facility of this kind north of Woods Hole at Cape Cod, Massachusetts.

"One of the many enticements for this concentration of brilliant scientists is the wide variety of aquatic life." Mrs. Sykes raised a pair of binoculars to her gold-rimmed prescription sunglasses and scanned the horizon without missing a beat. "Of course, the main reason most of you people are with us today is to see a whale or two. And I don't think we will disappoint." Mrs. Sykes lowered the binoculars and pointed offshore, past Piscatawk Island. "In a few minutes, we will be drawing alongside some turbulence that, I believe, will turn out to be a pod of our native sperm whales."

The engines continued cranking steadily toward their goal. The weather was cooperating, and even those previously blasé travelers were warming up to the idea of seeing the largest mammal on earth, up close and personal.

Mrs. Sykes chanted chapter and verse on the history of the whaling industry in North America as the ship ate up more and more distance.

"It was the development of the harpoon with exploding head that—" Mrs. Sykes paused and cleared her throat. She raised the binoculars to her eyes once again. " . . . that caused the ultimate—oh, *my*. *Oh, my*."

A little boy about the age of ten sneaked under the ex-teacher's arm and went to the rail for a better look.

"*Shark!*" he screamed in delight.

Ginny and Elizabeth crouched against the wind and bent over the flame. They exhaled in unison, and leaned against the brick wall of the hospital entrance to smoke in peace.

Dusk had given way to dark. The cigarette tips cast an eerie glow over the women's faces; both were sporting unflattering bags beneath their eyes, especially notable on Elizabeth's fair skin.

Martha Robson had staunchly refused to leave her husband's side, even during the lengthy MRI taken to detect any possible bleeding into Eamon's brain. Elizabeth was not allowed to accompany her friend into the testing room, and she could not bear to join her father and Claire Wallis—candy stripes and all—in the hospital coffee shop for respite.

Except for a quick trip to the Beer Barn for a carton of cigarettes, Elizabeth had paced for nearly ten hours straight, and it was showing.

"Eamon'll be all right," Ginny said.

"He has a tube in his throat."

"Respirator. He'll be all right," Ginny reiterated, more for her own benefit than for Elizabeth's.

"Maybe. Martha looks like death warmed over, though."

Ginny crushed her cigarette butt with her foot on the concrete next to the industrial ashtray.

"She won't leave." Ginny lit up again. "I even ordered her."

Elizabeth shook her head slowly.

"That never worked."

"Still doesn't. You might as well get on home, Biz. Take Frank with you. Claire has already put together a bed for Martha to spend the night."

"What a woman," Elizabeth commented dryly.

"Say what you will, Biz. She gets the job done."

"Couldn't have said it better, myself." Elizabeth pushed her cigarette deep into the kitty litter in the hospital ashtray. She rubbed her eyes and rotated her neck from side to side. "There's a horror-classic film festival on Channel 56 I've been looking forward to since date night, anyway."

"Good."

"I'll call Avis over to watch with me. Giving her the creeps has always made me feel better."

"Then I'll send Sandy over, too. You can have double the fun. She's a real cheap scream."

Elizabeth hugged her friend. "You're a real bud, Gin. I don't know why the criminal element says you have no sense of humor."

"Beats me. Now go home, and take Frank away from all this." As the electronic door opened for Elizabeth, Ginny spoke again. "Biz?"

"Yeah?"

"You been spottin' any sharks out around Piscatawk lately?"

"Sure. Makos. Want a barbecue?"

"Bigger than makos. Maybe twenty feet or more?"

Elizabeth searched Ginny's face for a sign of jest. "You

know these waters as well as I do. Are you pulling my leg? Why do you ask?"

"Had a spotting of what might be a great white from the *Pride of Dovekey* this afternoon," Ginny answered.

"Must be a mistake," Elizabeth shook her head again. "Tourists are always thinking they're caught up in a Steven Spielberg movie. Had a shark attack mayday on the radio once from some rag-boaters reporting a nuclear sub viciously docked up at the naval shipyard. I'll bet it was just a whale."

"Mrs. Sykes confirmed the sighting."

It was hard for Elizabeth to discount the opinion of her favorite science teacher, but she managed.

"I'd have to see it myself."

"Hope you don't, Biz. Mr. Elwell and I aren't set up for riot control." Ginny raised her hand tiredly in a good-bye. She opened the police cruiser door, and asked, "What time do you want Sandy over?"

"Eleven'd be good, if she's not too tired."

"*I'm* too tired. She'll be there, with popcorn." Ginny closed the car door and pulled away from the curb.

Frank and Claire were standing by the closed ICU door when Elizabeth returned. Ben Ryan was in the process of signing himself out.

"Go home and take your father with you," Ryan advised Elizabeth. "Claire is staying over to keep an eye on Martha."

And who will keep an eye on Claire? Elizabeth kept quiet. "Just about to, Doc." Elizabeth poked her father in the arm to get his attention. "Is Eamon going to be all right?"

"Don't know, Liz. You go home and get some sleep. Your friend may really need you tomorrow."

Elizabeth watched the old physician exit the hospital thinking how much she had not wanted to hear his advice. A green shade was drawn over the ICU door. The corridor was night quiet, except for the low hum of Claire Wallis's flirting.

Elizabeth jangled the spare truck keys at Frank, to whom she was still not speaking, and dragged herself out to the parking lot. She did not much care whether or not her father followed, but he did. Elizabeth drove with uncharacteristic caution back to the house.

The only good thing about the day was that it was nearly over.

Sandy and Avis straggled into the Will living room just as the local 11 o'clock news came on the television. Sandy was wide awake and feeling social. Avis, however, was a day person.

"I hate this," she groused to her sister. "You know I hate this, and I have a woodland walk I'm leading tomorrow morning for the Ladies' Guild. I'm the *leader,*" she emphasized. "I have to be *alert.*"

"For what?" Elizabeth asked, lowering her voice and wobbling the vibrato for effect. "The attack of the killer lady's slipper?"

"Stop it!" Avis warned.

"What?"

"That voice thing; you know what. That creepy voice thing you do just to scare me."

"I brought popcorn," Sandy offered brightly.

"You *love* popcorn," Elizabeth crooned, "and you love horror movies."

"No, suh."

"Yes, suh."

"No, su—"

"You two behave yourselves, or I'm coming in they'ah," Frank shouted from the kitchen.

Sandy squealed in a register high enough to call dogs. Petunia did not raise an ear, but it caused the distracted Elizabeth to jump a foot from the floor in fright. Avis laughed at the role reversal, then sobered quickly at what had made Sandy shout in the first place.

The film festival had not begun yet, but, more terrifying than Bela Lugosi, the television screen flickered the horrifying face of Dick Dawley, close-up and in living color. Elizabeth shot across the room on hands and knees to turn up the volume.

"Some are saying," The Dick-monster proclaimed to the newscaster on location, "that it's the old curse of Dovekey Beach. Well," he stared directly into the camera, "I say 'pshaw.' Just bad luck, that's all. . . . "

"Pshaw, my ass," Elizabeth said.

"Shhh," Avis hushed her sister.

"Shhh," Sandy hushed Avis.

"What the hell is going on?" Frank asked, carrying a large homemade pepperoni pizza baked on a cookie sheet, and a frosty six-pack of Pabst Blue Ribbon beer. "Am I going to have to separate you"—his eyes locked on the TV—"Woo, is that boy three-syllable ug-ul-y." He sat on the arm of his BarcaLounger and popped a beer to better listen.

" . . . dead bodies and shark attacks in Dovekey Beach," the disembodied voice of Dick Dawley continued. "We, right next do'ah at Pebble Beach, have not had one solitary incident of any death or injury." He smiled, then caught himself and stared soberly into the lens. Fade to black.

"Bastard!" Elizabeth cursed the screen as the news report moved on to the weather.

"Good to see you back to normal, Elizabeth," Frank said and handed his daughter a Pabst. "Pizza's gettin' cold," he advised.

And that's not all, Elizabeth thought.

Dick Dawley was a marked man.

SEVEN

THE HORIZON LINE was as crisp and sharp as a paper cut. The sun smiled down relentlessly on the glassy sheen of saltwater, as though to provoke a tantrum of steam from its placid surface.

The *Curmudgeon II* swung back in the direction of shore. It was a measure of Frank's guilt that he had humored Elizabeth's request to ship out beyond Piscatawk Island, five miles farther out than their usual run. To boot, Frank was doing the driving.

Elizabeth considered the possibility that things might be looking up.

"OCD," Frank shouted over the noise of the thirty-year-old engine to his daughter, sitting on the foot-wide rail a yard behind him. Elizabeth knew her father would elaborate without any prompting from her. "Obsessive/compulsive disorder. That," he slowed the boat and peered into the gray green water, "is when a person does something"—he pulled a stainless-steel .38 revolver from the back of his pants—"ov'ah, and ov'ah, and ov'ah—you did say Ginny wanted some mako to barbecue?—without there bein' any good reason to it." Frank throttled down again and took aim straight down the side of the lobster boat. *Blammm.* He fired once. "Damn, missed her."

"You trying to sink us?" Elizabeth asked calmly.

"No, suh, just trying to bag Ginny a mako."

"Ginny doesn't want a mako."

"Did she say not, or are you just bein' obsessive/compulsive again?"

"I am not obsessive/compulsive," she countered, wondering if she might be.

"They say it runs in families," Frank said, taking aim once more. *Blammm.*

"Oh, don't *even* go there."

"You been messin' with my gun? The sight appears t'be off a mite."

"You miss again?"

"No, suh. Just wanted to scare her." He tucked his gun back into his back belt. "Maybe scare up a great white so we can stop burnin' gas to hell and gone lookin' for one." Frank opened the throttle and aimed for home at a good ten knots to make his point.

"So now we're through. No man-eating sharks around here."

Frank pointed to the clam flats in the distance. "Want to get some back-up clams for the crate?" he asked.

"No, thank you."

"Like ridin' a horse, Lizzie. Best to crawl right back on," Frank advised.

"I do not have an unreasonable fear of finding another corpse, Father. I just"—she pointed to the sandbar herself—"do not like crowds." The small patch of sand was sprouting eight to ten humans. As they pulled closer, Elizabeth realized she had misjudged somewhat.

The clam flats had sprouted eight to ten Fish and Game officers, each one posting his or her very own "Flats Closed: The taking of clams prohibited until further notice. By order of NH F&G."

"I'll be damned!" Frank swore.

"I have no doubt whatsoever," Elizabeth agreed. She settled back onto her balance beam, one foot slung over the side to be splashed by the wake. The minute she got comfortable, there was a scramble from the khaki-suited entourage on the islet. "Oh, no," Elizabeth breathed. She was very much afraid that the uniforms had just discovered another body for Dick Dawley to throw on the fire.

Frank flipped on the marine radio and tuned into the Coast Guard frequency as he steered. All that came over the aged radio was an ear-shattering crackle. Elizabeth grabbed the side-window opening of the half-cabin and flung herself onto the bow of the boat. She knelt in the center of the wood, warm from the engine below, and snapped the eight-foot antenna upright. Frank swung the boat eastward and almost dropped her over the side before she got both sneakered feet inside.

"What the hell are you doing?" she shouted at Frank.

"Headin' out," he answered unnecessarily. The two small, but very fast, Fish and Game skiffs sped ahead of the doddering *Curmudgeon*. "There's a fire onboard the *Pride of Dovekey*. All available ships have been called out for evacuation."

"Oh, no!"

"You're repeating yo'ahself obsessively, Lizzie. Now crack me open a Pabst, would ya?"

Most of the yellow-rubber life rafts were empty by the time the *Curmudgeon* reached the black smoke that marked the location of the *Pride of Dovekey*. Frank slowly pulled up beside the power boat owned by The Eternal Sea Group. MacKay threw a line and pulled the ESG vessel astern.

"How many can you fit on board?" MacKay yelled.

Elizabeth did a quick surveillance and shouted back, "Eight. Make that seven."

MacKay turned his back to the wind and spoke into his marine-radio microphone. Then he turned his wheel over to a young woman in extremely short shorts, and jumped up onto the *Curmudgeon*.

"Okay, Liz. Hi, Frank. Just hold on here. The Coasties are towing a raft over here with six for you. He looked around the tub of lobsters in the center of the deck, eyes wandering over the debris and empty beer cans. "You have six more life jackets?"

"In the hold," Frank assured him and ducked below deck. One by one, an assortment of life preservers were thrown in Elizabeth's direction: Styrofoam, canvas, inflatable.

"Yard sales," Elizabeth explained. "Is anyone hurt?"

"Some smoke inhalation, but they've already been sent back to shore by speedboats." MacKay waved a violently orange Mae West to the approaching Coast Guard boat with a raft in tow. "The passengers you're transporting will be a little scared, and probably a lot pissed off—but no medical problems."

Elizabeth felt as though she had been kicked in the stomach.

"MacKay, God, you don't even know."

Frank resurfaced and threw a beer to MacKay, who caught it one-handed.

"What?" MacKay popped the can.

"Eamon Robson's been hospitalized," Elizabeth said and took a sip out of his beer.

"Shit!" MacKay spat and took back his Pabst. "Will he be out by Saturday?" The Coasties swung the life raft alongside the *Curmudgeon*. MacKay leaned over the side to help the first of the victims on board. Elizabeth steered the woman to a safe sitting position aft and handed her a flotation device. The next to come on was an impressively rotund gentleman who would require both Mackay and Elizabeth's muscle to hoist.

Elizabeth whispered into MacKay's ear.

"He may not come out, at all, Charles. Eamon's in critical condition." The fat man dangled precariously over open sea.

"He's what?"

"Keep your eyes on the boat, sailor," the Coast Guard ensign shouted.

"On the count of three," Elizabeth ordered. The couple yanked so efficiently, the large near-victim sprawled over the side and knocked the plastic lobster box and its contents from one end of the deck to the other. The woman at the back of the boat screamed as she was hit by a projectile three-pounder.

"*Mon Dieu!*" the fat man exclaimed.

"Chuck!" the cutesy short-short Barbie called from MacKay's boat. "We need you on board!"

"I'll bet," Elizabeth muttered.

"Frank, you help Liz. I gotta go. Liz, I'll call you later, okay?"

Elizabeth had not even said, "I'll bet," before MacKay was loading passengers onto the research vessel. She lifted three children into their waiting parents' arms before she needed help from Frank to steady a small, but elderly, man. The Wills had their quota. Elizabeth portioned out the life preservers, strapping the children into the newest models. Aside from some nasty smudging, everyone appeared unscathed.

Frank snatched the morning's catch from the curious fingers of the youngsters and threw the lobsters back into the holding tub. Elizabeth cast off to the ensign, who instructed her to go directly to the town dock, where emergency vehicles would be stationed.

At top speed, she headed home.

Now this, Elizabeth complained silently to herself, *is more than a coincidence.* What more could contribute to making her life hell?

"I'm calling my selectman!" Frank bellowed into her ear. "I demand to know why we got all French-Canadians!"

"*Fermez la bouche,*" Elizabeth enunciated, keeping her voice low.

Stragglers wheezed and puffed, perspiration soaking their hair and clothing. Those at the head of the group were not faring much better. Mosquitoes swarmed in a visible miasma, alighting only long enough to draw blood from their victims. Their bellies were so full that one wondered how they could remain airborne.

The heavy air smelled of moss and decay. The unprepared among the travelers added their own particular aroma to the lethargic wind. A little boy of ten years or so bore the markings of several battles lost with moldering stumps and swampy holes.

"I really hate this!" Avis griped under her breath.

"What, dear?" asked Claire Wallis, decked out in peach cotton Bermuda shorts and matching safari shirt.

"Nothing," Avis answered. For one of the first times in her life, she wished she were out on the ocean with her father and sister, rather than where she was: a mile out in the coniferous forest that marked off Dovekey Beach from its neighbors to the west.

The whole mess was Claire Wallis's fault. It was her brilliant idea to have the Ladies' Guild host informative little woodland walks to keep the beach-deprived busy and in town. Naturally, it was Frank Will who volunteered his younger daughter to help out. Avis promised herself to have Elizabeth make him pay for it, too. She smashed a lingering mosquito against her cheek.

"Jeremy!" a middle-aged woman called to her son. "Don't drink that!" She tried to get the hyperactive tyke to uncup his hands.

"Cool," he said and swung out of his mother's reach. "Look at the sea monkeys!" Jeremy ran over to Claire and Avis. "What are these *things* swimming around? They're sea monkeys, aren't they? Can I keep them? Will they grow up into real monkeys?"

Avis peered into the stagnant water in the boy's hands.

"Sure," Avis said. Immediately, she realized that the heat and stress were transforming her into her evil sister, and properly amended her misleading response. "But they won't turn into monkeys, sea or other."

"Why *not?*" the boy whined.

"Because," Avis reasoned in her very nice way, "those little things swimming around in your hands are mosquito larvae."

The haggard mother caught up, squealing.

"Cool," Jeremy said. His mother captured him by his shirt-tail and shook his hands, spraying everyone within a ten-foot diameter with brackish water and future mosquitoes. His enthusiasm undampened, Jeremy took off like a bullet into the underbrush.

"Don't worry," Claire reassured the frantic mother. "We're miles from the ocean here. He'll be just fine. Nothing to worry about."

The mother appeared properly dubious.

"Jeremy is a champion swimmer," she contended.

It was Claire's turn to be dubious.

Ben Ryan scribbled into the chart hanging at the end of Eamon Robson's hospital bed. The shush-shush of the respirator was the only sound in the small room. Martha Robson watched the doctor with red-rimmed eyes. Her ash-blond hair hung lank around her face.

"The MRI was negative, Martha," he said. "That's good news. No hemorrhaging. No tumor." He walked to where Martha was sitting and put a kindly hand on her shoulder. She looked nearly as unwell as her comatose husband. She did not respond to Dr. Ryan's hollow reassurance. "I think you should get some rest, Martha. When Eamon comes out of this, he's going to need you to be strong."

Martha lifted her eyes to the doctor's. "Please don't patronize me, Dr. Ryan. I am not a child anymore. I have not been for a good long time."

Ryan withdrew his hand. He knew she was right about that. Still, when a doctor cares for an entire community, he tends to set his patients permanently into an unyielding time frame. With Martha Drake, that would have been around age seventeen.

"I'm going to write you a prescription for a mild sedative, Martha Ann. The nurse will fill it for you at the hospital pharmacy."

"No, thank you."

"I insist. Take the medication or not, as you choose. But you don't look very well, Martha. I think you should."

"I know, Dr. Ryan. I know you do." She closed her eyes in dismissal.

Ben Ryan let himself out of the close quarters and into the relatively fresh air of the corridor. A quiver of guilt worked its way down the old man's spine. He tried to blame it on arthritis.

He could not.

The fifteen middle-to-older-aged woodland warriors struggled to maintain interest. According to the schedule, they would only have to endure another half-hour or so.

Claire Wallis pointed out every clump of trillium, lily of the valley, mayflower, and lady's slipper en route. They were arduously following the stone wall that would lead back to old Route 1 and the comforts of civilization. It had been so long since any native had regularly wandered this patch of woods that the old pathway had all but disappeared. Mother Nature had reclaimed her space in spades.

Avis knew that as long as the adventurers had the wall to follow, they were in no danger of becoming lost, but Claire was fit to be tied when they found they had wandered away from the old trail. The late Mr. Wallis had been an attorney, and Claire had survived him with an unnatural fear of litigation.

"In the spring," Avis struggled to find something to talk about other than wild orchids, "before they open, these ferns can be collected and cooked." An elderly woman feigned interest, so Avis muddled along. "They're called 'fiddleheads,' and they sell for a lot of money in the city."

"That's true," the little old lady agreed.

Bless her, Avis thought.

"*Jeremy!*" the urchin's mother screeched too near Avis's ear. "*Jeremy!* You come out of hiding now. Mommy's not seeking!" She reached out and grasped Avis's arm. "We're almost back, aren't we?" She stumbled over a root and fell into Avis.

"Yes. Almost home. Another mile or so."

"*Jer-e-meeeee!* We're almost home. Come *out* now!"

Claire whispered nervously to her co-leader, "I hope the child hasn't gotten himself lost."

Avis was not hoping that hard, but when she thought about the hours it would take to find the little monster, she started sweeping the undergrowth with her eyes.

"Oh, look"—Claire pointed to the right of the stone wall for the benefit of the sightseers—"that's princess pine. Not pine at all, of course, and protected by the state. When I was a child," she went on, "we used to collect it and wind it into wreaths and garland decorations on banisters and such during the Christmas season."

Avis squinted into the woods and lagged to allow the tour

to pass her. She spotted a movement fifteen feet into the dense foliage.

"Jeremy, honey," she called, low enough not to attract undue attention from his mother. "Jeremy, if you come out, I'll show you something really cool." What, she had no idea, but she had not reached the stage of frustration where she would implement the old never-fail ice-cream-on-the-way-home trick. Unkindly, she thought the little boy was quite heavy enough, thank you. "Jeremy?"

The boy's scream bounced from tree to tree.

His mother knocked herself and Claire Wallis to the forest floor in her hysteria. Avis leaped in the direction of the child's voice, ripping the bejesus out of the right knee of her new L. L. Bean khakis on a ragged branch.

"Here! Come *here!*" Jeremy yelled.

From ahead, Avis heard his mother call, "Mommy's coming, darling. Mommy's coming right now!" accompanied by the sound of crashing limbs and unsure feet.

Avis ducked under a treacherous branch. A splash of daylight shimmered on what had long ago been the trail. She could barely make out the boy's blond head through the dense vegetation. She damned her father to hell and slogged through a slimy puddle hidden beneath a pillow of fallen leaves.

"*Hurry!*" came the boy's voice.

Avis picked up as much speed as she could, bent double and steering wet shoes through a tangle of vines and wild blackberries.

"Hurry, Avis!" Claire called from behind. "We'll catch up with you."

She broke through from the trees into the small clearing. Jeremy stood up and waved innocently. Aside from a layer of grime, the child seemed in perfect health. Animated, even.

"It's all right, guys," Avis shouted to the group. "He's fine."

"I found the trail!" he added loudly. "I found it all by my-self! And guess what *else?*"

Avis could not imagine, nor did she wish to.

"What, honey?" the mother-from-the-center-of-the-earth crooned from afar. "What have you discovered?"

Discipline? Avis wondered. If he were one of her own tribe, she'd show him several new worlds before the afternoon was over. Since he was not, blessedly, the fruit of her loins, she contented herself with a slow boil as she approached him. She ambled to allow the mother to arrive in time to intervene.

Claire led the other woman out of the greenery five yards farther up the path.

Jeremy lunged to the ground, grabbed something, and took off at a trot toward his mother.

"Look, Mommy, it's a *snake!*"

"Put that nasty thing down, Jeremy, this instant!" his mother ordered.

Oh, God, save this poor child from me, Avis prayed. She was only three long steps away and could rescue the poor reptile, but who would rescue the brat from her?

"Do as your mother says!" Claire shouted. Both of the older women were winded and not making great progress.

"But I *love* snakes," Jeremy teased, lifting the creature to his mouth.

Avis wished Elizabeth were along for the festivities. Her older sister still could not resist catching whatever unsuspecting garter snake she stumbled across. Avis hated the musky smell they deposited on her hands, no matter what gardeners had to say about how helpful they were to have around.

"Give me the snake, Jeremy," she said as moderately as she could manage.

"Nuh-uh," Jeremy shook his head and puckered up. "I'm going to kiss my new friend, Mr. Snake."

Avis reached out, hoping adrenaline would not cause her to accidentally injure Mr. Snake.

"*Ow!*" Jeremy mewled. He threw the snake over his head and nearly into Avis's hand. "Mommy, it *bit* me!"

Claire burst upon the scene.

"Kill it!" she ordered Avis.

Avis looked down at her feet where the stunned snake lay, thinking she'd like to kiss it herself. Then she understood Claire's unusual vehemence. The object of Jeremy's affection was not a black snake with yellow stripes. It was a bit too long and far too brown to be a garter snake. Against her nature and very fiber, Avis raised her booted foot and crushed the reptilian head beneath her heel. Later, she would swear that she could feel the crushing of its delicate bones through her shoe.

She did not need to inspect the mutilated thing any closer. She knew that, somehow, Jeremy-from-hell had gotten himself bitten by a rare—at least at lower elevations—native timber rattler.

Cars were parked bumper-to-bumper in the parking lot and scattered like discarded toys on the roadway shoulder. At the ER entrance, the Dovekey Beach ambulance vied for space with the larger Pebble Beach emergency vehicle.

Avis deserted her Jeep in the circular drive and carried the crying child at a dead run into the waiting room. His face had swollen during the short drive and turned an alarming red. She elbowed herself and her charge through the unprecedented number of people in the small room toward the nurses' station. A few feet down the hallway, she spotted the balding head of Ben Ryan.

"Doc!" Avis called, oblivious to the congestion. "This kid got himself bitten by a rattlesnake."

Frank Will walked a very fat man out of the examination room to Avis's right, and said, "Well, I doubt tha'hell outta that." Dr. Ryan pushed Avis and Jeremy into the vacated space.

"Put him on the gurney, Avis," he ordered and called to a nurse for help.

"Yes, suh," Avis defended herself. She reached into her extra-deep khaki pocket.

"No, suh," Frank argued.

"Yes, *suh,*" Avis insisted and pulled the snake carcass out for Frank's inspection.

Ben Ryan glanced over and said, "Yes, suh, Frank. Go fetch me a nurse and tell her what we've got he'ah. There's antivenin in the refrigerator. Bring it with you. Avis, when did this happen?"

"Not fifteen minutes, yet, Doc. Would have gotten him sooner, but I had to pull his mother off and run him through the woods."

"Good girl." He inspected the dual fang punctures.

"New England timber rattlers aren't that poisonous, are they, Doc?" Avis asked. The boy wailed in pain.

"Nope"—he patted the child's head and did a quick check for fever—"but this is something of a nasty location. Understand?"

Avis nodded. Frannie, the triage nurse, pulled Avis from the examination area, and handed Ryan a syringe and vial of serum. Avis backed directly into her sister.

"What the hell is going on, Biz?"

"Nice talk," Frank commented from over her shoulder. Jeremy's mother barged into the Will contingent.

"Where's Jeremy? Where's my baby?"

"Right in there, Mrs. uh," Avis pointed, and was nearly knocked to the linoleum for her trouble. Her question was lost in the din of crying and wails. In less than a minute, Ben Ryan poked his head out from behind the privacy curtain and spoke to the Will family.

"Elizabeth," he said, "you absolutely have got to get Martha away from here. I don't care what it takes, but she has got to get some rest."

"Is she all right?"

"You tell me, later, okay? I've got my hands full at the moment." The curtain snapped closed.

Avis and Elizabeth nodded to one another and strode directly into the ICU. They were shocked by Martha's appearance, though they were both too well-bred to say so—even to one another.

It required ridiculously little effort to steer Martha Robson away from her husband's bedside and into Avis's black Jeep. Their old friend, supported between the two sisters, felt as brittle as old paper. Both knew the doctor to be right about getting her away from the chaos at the hospital. Martha did not utter a word during the entire trip back to the Wild Rose.

Miss Locke appeared on the verge of fainting at the sight of her guest, but, as could be expected, rallied immediately.

"Miss Locke," Elizabeth asked after Martha was properly tucked into the cast-iron bed upstairs, "I hate to ask, but could you keep an eye on Martha for a bit? Doc Ryan is worried about her, and Avis and I have something we just have to do."

"Of course, girls. Of course. You don't worry about a thing. I'll check up on her every five minutes. As soon as I finish my chores, I'll sit with her. Will that be all right?"

"Wonderful. Thank you, Miss Locke." Elizabeth pulled a small brown bottle from her shirt pocket. "Doc Ryan would like you to try to get her to take one of these. Instructions are on the bottle. I couldn't get her to swallow one; maybe you'll have more influence."

"I'll try, dear. Now, don't worry. We'll be fine."

Elizabeth insisted on driving back to the area of woods where the snake had been discovered. Avis was so wrung out that she did not even protest reflexively. As Elizabeth chronicled the *Pride of Dovekey* disaster, Avis covered her eyes with her hands and sank deeper into the passenger seat.

After the frantic stomping Avis had done getting Jeremy back to the road, it was no problem to retrace the way back to the snake's lair.

"You ever see a rattler around here, Avis?"

"Nope."

"Me, neither," Elizabeth said, poking the path with a dry stick. "A couple of times in the White Mountains, that's all."

"Well, Dad always said we had them around here, too."

"Ayuh. And just like his claim to the Rumanian throne, it's a possibility." The stick turned up a scalp of loosened moss. Elizabeth clapped her hands sharply three times to warn any slumbering danger of her intent, and knelt by the dislodged growth. She placed her palm on the furry thatch. "Avis, feel this."

"It's warm. Wicked warm."

"Ayuh," Elizabeth agreed and lifted the greenery, raking the underlying compost with her fingers. Beneath the dark soil was a bed of egg-sized granite rocks. "What does this remind you of?" she asked her sister.

"A clambake," Avis answered. Elizabeth nodded.

"Someone planted that rattler, and built it a nice, warm bed so it wouldn't move away into the woods. Right in the middle of the trail.

"That's sick."

"Ayuh."

"I don't even *know* anyone that sick," Avis protested.

"Yes, suh."

"No, suh."

"Yes, suh."

"Oh," Avis conceded. She guessed that they both *did* know someone sick enough to booby-trap a walkway. "You can't prove it, Biz. Get Ginny to check it out."

"Oh, sure. Maybe she can dust the moss for fingerprints or something. Ginny's got more than she can handle right now, anyway." Elizabeth stood up and wiped off her bare knees.

"What can you do?" Avis asked.

"Squeeze a confession out of the little pustule."

Miss Locke was called away to check out half her guests that afternoon. She was unsurprised that most of her reservations chose to cancel and vacation elsewhere. On the brighter side—and there always was one, in Miss Locke's opinion—she could hold off making up some of the rooms until Rose returned. Martha Drake needed her attention more than her business did.

No amount of cajoling could convince Martha to take the sedative Doc Ryan had prescribed. Miss Drake had gotten a dry English muffin and a cup of rose-hip tea down the young woman's throat, but that was all she could accomplish. Martha would not speak, nor cry. Miss Locke was concerned enough that she very nearly shooed her departing guests out the front door.

Martha was strangely content to lie awake in the beautiful bedroom. One of the elderly sisters had placed a large arrangement of daylilies next to the bed. The iridescent orange blossoms lasted only one day, but were evenly replaced with new openings on the next.

Martha wondered if Eamon would be back beside her in that room before the dormant buds had all dropped from the slender stems.

Her long-held belief system would not allow her to think otherwise. From earliest childhood, Martha had been taught her manners well. She was universally recognized as considerate and thoughtful to a fault.

In a daze, she padded her way down the back stairs and into the Wild Rose's kitchen. When Eamon was returned to her—as he surely would be—he should have everything he loved. He would have her, and a fresh jar of wild rose-hip jelly.

The pantry was well-stocked with a collection of sparkling canning jars. She chose two of the smaller sizes, thinking how pleased Eamon would be to see that she had been thinking of him.

Having at last accomplished something useful, Martha finally fell into a deep sleep.

Miss Locke was so relieved to see Martha resting, she, too, dozed in the bright bedroom, over a book of poetry by Celia Thaxter.

Elizabeth's eyes were locked on the ceiling of her room. She had tried closing them, but still had not been able to drift off to sleep. The bedside clock read 2:14 A.M. She got out of the mussed sheets, dislodging old yearbooks and photographs from where she had left them to fall onto the braided rug, and went downstairs to the kitchen.

She tore a piece of paper from the roll that hung by the door and scrawled a quick note, somewhat amazed at herself. To her further amazement, she found herself hungry and started a quick food reconnoitering.

Petunia heard the opening of the refrigerator door and materialized from Frank's room on the first floor. Elizabeth looked down at the tubby animal.

"The last thing you need is a midnight snack."

Petunia performed her only trick, snapping into full sit-up. Owing to her ballast, she could remain in that position for, well,

Elizabeth did not know. Petunia always got thrown something edible before she fell over.

Elizabeth tossed the cocker spaniel a piece of liverwurst and cracked the freezer. There were dozens of plastic containers of lobster stew and three microwavable burritos. She poured herself a shot of bourbon.

If she did not get drowsy by dawn, she would keep drinking. She had promised Avis only that she would wait until the next day.

What she had to do might better be done drunk, anyway.

EIGHT

FRANK READ THE note before making himself breakfast. Being alone, except for Petunia, he allowed himself the luxury of a worried look.

Elizabeth's junk pile of an MGB was not in the driveway, nor could he see it parked down the hill at the gallery. She must have had to jump-start the old jalopy by popping the clutch on her way down the slope, he thought. Otherwise, the machine's tubercular coughing would have wakened him. There was nothing devious about it.

It happened three mornings out of four.

What never, but never, happened was Elizabeth's calling in sick. Frank picked up the note for another read. She wasn't sick. She was taking a mental-health day. Whatever. She had not missed a morning run in five years.

Frank allowed himself another scowl.

Mental-health day?

There was never a Will born who had any use for mental health.

"Wouldn't know what to do with it," Frank told Petunia, who agreed with anything Frank said.

It was for two very sound reasons that Elizabeth drove with a vengeance.

One, if she stopped the car for a light or sign, she was not certain she could coax the MG back into action. Fortunately, there were enough back and side roads to get her where she was going without risking a mechanical failure.

Two, vengeance.

Every turn of logic Elizabeth had taken during her long, sleepless night led her to the same greasy spot. And that place was the tourist industry.

She had been thrown off course for a while by Eamon Robson's critical condition. He was not a native, but he was married to a local girl. If it was visitors only who were being targeted for injury, he should have gotten some kind of immunity by virtue of his marriage to a Drake. Hurting him would be like hurting a neighbor. At least that was Elizabeth's take, and it had won her prime suspect an extra hour of safety.

Elizabeth ran everyone in the area through her mind to try and get a grasp on a motivation, including Charles MacKay. In fact, he was the most logical choice. His attitude toward boating enthusiasts whipping up the waters around his research compound was notorious. The locals avoided the ocean around Piscatawk Island just to save themselves copious grief and aggravation.

Of course, it would be impossible for MacKay to forcibly relocate the whole community after an existent three-hundred-and-fifty years, but relatively simple to start weeding out the transients on a more manageable day-to-day basis. And she had only his word that the medical waste was untraceable to his well-equipped lab.

But, then, the list turned back to Eamon Robson. MacKay certainly had the opportunity and the motivation. Except for one self-esteem-lowering thing that Elizabeth knew of.

Rugby.

If MacKay had a list of priorities—and she was sure he did; the anal retentive not-available-Saturday-nights crud—the game of rugby came second, after his work at The Eternal Sea Group. She did not even waste a second pondering her own possible rating. She was morosely convinced that it was a sliding scale, anyway.

MacKay needed Eamon to play flanker for the Piscatawk Pirates. He would have thrown himself into a tuna net to protect the chance of his team defeating Amoskeag for the first time ever, and that shot in the dark was a ringer: Eamon Robson.

Scratch MacKay.

The entire puzzle hinged somehow on Eamon Robson. He was the crimp in the rope, and the straight line as well.

Which brought Elizabeth around to her second choice, and that all hung on Martha Robson, the Cod Queen. Everyone loved Martha. And some more than others.

The picture of senior-prom night flashed like lightning before Elizabeth's eyes. It had been a triple date. Ginny and Fuzzy Aubertine, Martha and basketball Captain Thorpe What's-his-name; and Elizabeth and (ugh) Dick Dawley.

They had all had a perfectly miserable time.

Ginny was probably hovering on the ledge of discovery that she was not very interested in living the rest of her life with a man, so her big evening was a lot more platonic than Fuzzy had envisioned. He mostly sulked his way through the momentous evening.

What's-his-name's father was being shipped out of Pease Air Force Base to some godforsaken settlement in Texas a week before graduation, which did nothing to cheer him or Martha up. For the most part, they mooned at one another.

And Elizabeth's last-ditch date was madly in love with her friend, Martha Drake. Worst, Dawley got himself sauced enough to cry on his date's shoulder about it.

Funny, how one forgets all the details, Elizabeth thought. *Ha. Ha. But then it all comes back up on you, like gas.*

Elizabeth was drawn by the television cameras and the crowd, like a tornado to a trailer park. She pulled the MG into a parallel slot pitched down on a steep hill to ensure her exit. She wanted it to be a good one.

Putting good manners aside, she elbowed her way through the gawkers. Sidewalk vendors had set up early to make a little hay while the sun was shining. Guests from the shanty cabins and Eastern Bloc–inspired condominiums basked in the reflected glow of national attention. Several held up signs saying hello to relatives from Halifax to Honduras. Out of habit, Elizabeth paused at the fringe of the crowd, and then she got over herself and plunged forward into camera range.

Dick Dawley was so fascinated by what he was saying to the American public, his reflexes were slow.

Elizabeth pinched two inches of flab at the back of his belt before he could make a defensive move to protect himself. If it were not for his false pride, he would have howled like the dog Elizabeth considered him to be.

The newswoman interviewing Dawley was a pro. Without skipping a beat, she filled the dead air.

"And this is . . . ?"

"Lizzie," Dick grimaced. "Elizabeth Will. A resident of the beleaguered"—one eyelid dropped—"of the village of Dovekey Beach."

"Welcome," offered the impeccably groomed brunette with the Pepsodent smile, "and what do you think of the reemergence of the curse of Dovekey Beach? Is this yet another black period in the history of your small town?"

"Unless you count Dick, here, there has never been a curse on Dovekey Beach." Elizabeth considered taking back her statement or amending it to make it less litigious, but let it stand. Let the pageant queen deal with it.

Dawley jumped in. "She's such a kidder. We've been friends for years. Close friends. Why, Lizzie was my date to—"

Elizabeth cut him off rather than have the havoc she planned to wreak on his person broadcast to a potential jury pool.

"This has been blown out of proportion. I'll bet Pebble Beach has had its share of accidents, too, hasn't it, Dick?" She did not pause for a denial. "Our chief of police, Lavinia Philbrick, has everything under control."

"Unfortunately," the newscaster picked up, "Chief Philbrick has not been available for comment. And there you have it. Coincidence or conspiracy at Dovekey Beach? This is Maddie MacDonald, live for Boston Channel Five."

The news team dispersed and took the rubberneckers with them. Elizabeth took Dick in her pincer hold off to a yellow-jacket–swarmed trash bin and released him.

"What do you—" he started.

"Shut up, Dick. I mean it." He knew she did. "I know you are responsible for what's happening in Dovekey, you piece of mercenary gull shit. And as soon as I can prove it, I'm going to have your sorry ass thrown in jail. You hear me? But until I get the goods on you, knock it off. Because we're going to be watching every move you make from here on in."

"Why would I—" Dawley stopped himself, knowing full well why he would. "I haven't done a damned thing, Liz. Whatever is happening in Dovekey has nothing to do with me."

"Bull!"

"It doesn't. I'll admit it's made some good press for us here, but I'm innocent of anything beyond advancing commerce."

He looked so sincere that Elizabeth hesitated, but not long enough for Dick's taste.

"Oh, give me a break," she recovered. "Are you denying that you're in love with Martha Drake? Because I know better. And I know you, you slime bucket. For all I know, the rest of the accidents in Dovekey were nothing but a smoke screen to cover your real intention to kill off Martha's husband. Don't even insult me by pretending you're not smarmy enough."

"Is *this* what it's all about?" Dawley leaned against the trash can and was warned off by the wasps. Instead, he sat on the seawall. "You're still jealous. I should have known." He shook his head sagely. Elizabeth began to stutter, and locked her lips tightly together until she had regained control.

"Watch your back, Dick," she warned when she was finally able, and stormed back to where she had parked her car. Dawley watched her, arms crossed, pleased as punch.

The parking lot of Vinnie Bartlett's Breakfast 'n' Beans was full, as usual, but Elizabeth needed some sustenance to calm her enraged stomach and soul. The dining room was mobbed with locals, bemoaning the murder of what had looked like a banner fiscal season. Vinnie was just bemoaning in general.

"I can't believe it," he complained. "Height of the season, and I got *three* cabinettes vacant. Three. Goes against nature."

"Eggs over easy, bacon crisp, and a short stack," Elizabeth ordered.

"Can you believe it? Coffee black, right? One guy croaks and my business goes down the crapper."

"More than one, Vinnie," Elizabeth corrected. "And may I have the *real* maple syrup?"

"Don't you always get the real stuff?" Vinnie asked, aggrieved. "Locals always get real maple syrup. It's a rule."

A rule made because only the locals could tell the difference, and Vinnie's staff did not want to bother making two trips. Nonetheless, Elizabeth resolved not to take her suspicious nature out on poor Vinnie. Over the years, he had sent a lot of business her way. Some summers, her *only* business.

As always happened at peak hours, the nonsmoking section of Vinnie's became nonexistent. Elizabeth was reminded that she had picked up the filthy habit again, and lit up. The blast of nicotine may have annoyed the spit out of her cardiovascular system, but it did a world of good for her nerves. Halfway down the cigarette, Vinnie returned with Elizabeth's breakfast.

"Enjoy," he ordered, and placed a small unopened jar of preserves next to her coffee. "Folks keep leaving crap in their rooms. Personally, I can't stomach the stuff." It was a jar of Miss Locke's famous rose-hip jelly. "Anyway, Frank will eat anything."

"Thanks, Vinnie." Elizabeth took a forkful of egg to her mouth. Albumen slid from between the prongs back onto her plate. One of these days, Vinnie was going to have to learn how to cook.

Sated, she paid her bill and left Vinnie an extra dollar. No reason for everyone in town to go on public assistance.

Frank was in agreement.

"You on welfare, or what?" he asked when Elizabeth walked into the gallery. He was knitting heads for his traps behind the framing counter.

"How was the run?" Elizabeth asked. She placed Vinnie's gift to Frank in front of him and went into the back room to grab a pair of grungy sneakers that were tossed in a corner.

"Oh, *now* you care," Frank answered. "The usual. Maybe a few over what's to be expected, not that there's any market around these parts lately."

"You busy?"

"Do I look busy?"

"Thank you for watching the gallery." She kissed her father on the cheek. Frank acted as though it was the sort of thing she did all the time. "I'm going back out. Does the *Curmudgeon* need any gas?"

"Nope." Frank threw her a set of keys. "Take the truck. Want to make su'ah you get back. If I'm not around when you get he'ah, I'll be at an emergency town-council meetin'. You might want to be the'ah. Claire's picking me up at seven."

"Then I'll try to make it."

"Thought you might," Frank said, and returned to his handiwork. He could read his daughter like a comic book.

The three women huddled together over the table in companionable silence. Six soft, heavily veined hands worked in perfect harmony. The white plastic egg timer dinged from the stove.

"I hope that didn't disturb Martha Ann," Miss Locke worried aloud. She left her place and donned an embroidered oven mitt before opening the stove door.

"She was sleeping like a baby when I looked in on her," Claire said.

"Relief," Rose Sykes offered. Miss Locke removed a large tray of homemade scones from the oven, and slid the hot tray to the far end of the counter by the sink. "Those smell lovely, Sissy," she added.

"Eamon really *is* better, isn't he, Claire?" Miss Locke asked.

"I said so, didn't I? I checked on him personally at the beginning of my shift at the hospital, and again at the end. He's still in intensive care, but Ben is confident that he can be taken off the respirator tomorrow at the latest."

"That is comforting," said Rose. Claire nodded agreement.

"I might shade the truth a bit to comfort Martha, but I most assuredly would not lie to you."

"Of course not," Miss Locke agreed. "Now, I think we're way ahead in getting ready for teatime. As soon as the scones cool, we'll be finished."

"I think we made too many," Rose said. "We don't have many guests left."

Claire placed a small arrangement of fresh flowers in the center of the silver tray. "Everything will be all right." She was the detail person, as always.

"Yes," Miss Locke agreed. "Scones freeze beautifully."

Piscatawk Island grew larger on the horizon. Elizabeth took care not to increase her speed as she approached. The seven-mile trip was supposed to accomplish more than one thing. She was not sure exactly how many items she could tick off her list, but number one was a shark watch by an experienced eye.

But if there was a shark around, Elizabeth had not seen it. Not so much as a mako. She did spot a powerboat headed from the research center directly for the *Curmudgeon,* though.

It was Ginny. Elizabeth throttled down to wait for her friend. Something must have been up for Ginny to find the two hours it took to make the round trip.

"What the hell were you thinking?" Ginny shouted before she had even thrown a line to Elizabeth.

"What?" Elizabeth tied the police skiff to the bobbing lobster boat and pulled it in closer.

"That damned piece of work with Dick Dawley this morning."

"Word travels fast."

"What?" Ginny yelled. Elizabeth shut the *Curmudgeon*'s engine down.

"I said"—Elizabeth leaned over the rail—"word travels fast."

"So do restraining orders. Dawley got a judge to issue one against you before you even got back to work. Your father accepted service, by the way."

"I will try to smooth the shock from my face."

"And while we're on the subject of you keeping your nose out of other people's business, what are you doing out here?"

"Visiting my boyfriend?"

"You," Ginny accused, "are too old to have a boy-anything. Now, you let me do my job, Biz."

"It just occurred to me—"

"Well, it occurred to me, too, lady. My hands are full enough as it is without having to worry about you."

"Don't. That was the point. You're busy enough. I thought I'd help out."

"Yeah, well, that's what Mr. Elwell gets the big bucks for. Take a time out."

"Okay." Elizabeth agreed far too readily for Ginny's taste. She cast the police skiff off.

"I mean it, Biz. If I have to, I'll put you under house arrest. Think about it." Ginny fired up the twin motors. "Locked up for days at a time with Frank."

"Police brutality," Elizabeth protested, restarting the *Curmudgeon*'s engine. "It's a conspiracy!" she shouted and made her way to the Piscatawk dock.

After some wandering, she finally located MacKay, holed up in his smaller, private laboratory at the far end of the facility. His graduate students had taken off in the research vessel to do God-only-knew-what without being scrutinized under the watchful eye—currently glued to the eyepiece of a microscope— of their mentor. That was fine with Elizabeth. The longer she was out of college, the more college-aged people annoyed her.

"No, please," she said, coming up behind him. "Don't bother to get up."

124

"I thought you were busy with the local media. What are you doing here?"

"What are *you* doing?"

"Dinoflagellate peeping."

"I wondered what you did all by yourself out here."

"Give up?"

"Yes." Elizabeth pulled a stool next to him. "What is a dinoflagellate?"

He pushed away from the mechanism to allow Elizabeth a closer look.

"Cellular dinoflagellates are the little buggers that carry the disease you know as 'red tide.' "

"Seafood paralytic poisoning," she muttered, squinting into the lens. "Don't patronize me. I went to U.N.H. Life sciences."

"Then leave both eyes open and prove it, or you'll go blind."

"Thank you, Doctor. What exactly am I looking for?"

"Specifically, *Gonyaulax catenella.*"

"Gesundheit! Am I seeing it?"

"I would not dare to venture." He tapped her shoulder to move away. "But they're there."

"You're patronizing me again." Elizabeth stood and stretched her aching back. "They're always there. Are they in a concentration that is dangerous?"

"Shush. I'm counting."

"That's why Ginny was out here!"

"Shush."

"She brought you these samples. But from where?" Elizabeth wandered to the window and fiddled with a plastic bag. "From the clam flats, of course."

"Brilliant deduction, my dear Will. Care to deduce further?"

"Concentration is not high enough to poison a French-Canadian."

"Blahhh!" MacKay imitated the sound of a game-show mistake buzzer. "Wrong. As you will no doubt inform me you already know, persons with no built-up resistance can be mildly poisoned from a very small dose. But you happen to be right that the levels are not sufficiently high to warrant the closing of the clam flats."

"MacKay?"

"Yes?"

Elizabeth threw the plastic bag she had been fingering onto the lab table.

"You have not touched this medical waste I asked you to look at, have you?"

"As a matter of fact, no."

"Well, as a matter of fact, why not?"

MacKay heaved a sigh and rubbed his eyes. "Because, between the Fish and Game boys, the State Police, and Ginny Philbrick, I have been analyzing myself into a stupor. And, in case you hadn't noticed before, I am not especially the civic-minded type."

"Not your choice."

"Bingo!" MacKay stood and stretched. "But a man has got to eat, even in a forced-labor camp. Since you're here, anyway, why don't the two of us raid the dining-hall refrigerator?"

"Yum. Leftover cafeteria food."

"I'll make you a deal. Let me shower, and I'll even heat it up for you." He kissed Elizabeth perfunctorily and rapped her on the arm.

"Go," she said. "I'll amuse myself with the dino-whoosits."

"Don't open anything."

"I won't. Go. I'm starving."

He went.

Elizabeth turned the plastic bag over in her hands, careful not to get pricked on the sharp needles inside. Bored already, she walked back to the window. In the light, a syringe that had loosed itself from a bit of gauze twinkled in the sunshine.

Well, that's wrong, Elizabeth thought. A twinkling hypo is definitely wrong. She trotted to the door, opened it, and glanced down the hall. MacKay had disappeared. She closed and locked the door.

Daintily, with thumbs and forefingers, Elizabeth unsealed the bag, then worked the slide from the microscope stage. She put it aside with great care. With greater care, she reached into the bag and extracted one of the syringes.

Holding the plunger end with one hand, she slid the tip of the needle into the microscope and bent over for a quick look. Then she took another quick look.

The needle was clean. By pushing forward, she got a documentary-style view of the length of the hypodermic. She was no professional, but had suffered through enough lab courses in college to know when something was damned near sterile.

She kept her ears open for a sign of MacKay's unexpected return as she inspected every piece of debris she had packaged for MacKay. They were all clean; bandages, cotton balls, and needles. So much for MacKay's explanation why someone would dump medical waste, let alone where it came from.

Elizabeth unlocked the lab door and opened it just as the very damp Charles MacKay was reaching for the exterior knob. He immediately surveyed his lab.

"I knew it. I knew you couldn't behave yourself." He lifted the water-sample slide and reinserted it into the microscope. He took a look to make sure the sample had not been adulterated by Elizabeth's meddling and said, "It's my own fault. Fortunately, no harm done. Now, let's eat."

"There's another problem."

"Spare me."

"The waste I gave you to look at hasn't been used. It's *clean*."

"That's not a problem, Liz."

"Yes, it is. I mean, it's good that no one was put in any real danger. The problem is motivation. That bag isn't filled with medical waste, it's just medical *stuff*. Dovekey Beach only has one doctor. This junk was dumped on the state beach for the sole purpose of scaring away the tourists."

"Well, it worked. So? You're not accusing Doc Ryan, are you?"

"Of course not. But I know someone on the hospital board with access to syringes. So, can't Dick Dawley be prosecuted for it?"

MacKay took Elizabeth by the arm and led her out of the room. "Only if he's guilty. Even then, I don't think they'll give him the chair." He steered her out of the smaller building and down a walkway to the communal hall. "Think scientifically for a moment, Will.

"You are trying to tie this man into a series of accidents, deaths, and illnesses that have occurred over the past week. Right?"

"You bet."

"We don't even know that the three deaths can be attributed to anything but good, old-fashioned natural causes." MacKay opened a large industrial refrigerator and pulled out a container of milk and a tray of cold cuts. "I mean, we don't have any documentation to the contrary, do we?"

"The way you said that was very revealing, MacKay."

"Okay"—he pulled a loaf of bread off a far counter—"so the young woman's death was suspicious. Ben Ryan sent blood samples away for further testing, but he says accidental. The two old people, too, but only to confirm that their deaths were natural. And before you start nagging, we can't perform those tests here. We're a marine facility."

"Dinoflagellates R Us, huh?" Elizabeth dropped several

128

slices of boiled ham between two pieces of white bread and took a bite.

"Precisely." MacKay leaned against the counter. "And don't forget patience being a virtue and all those Puritan homilies. Now, what time is your curfew, little girl?"

The audience participants at town hall were standing-room only, and hotter than pantyhose in hell.

Asa Fleck had remembered to send out the notices, but had neglected to open the windows during the afternoon, and the July heat hung like a damp blanket over the residents of Dovekey Beach, despite the open double doors facing the parking lot and pastoral cemetery beyond. New England conservativeness precluded such fripperies as air conditioning in public buildings, and public opinion marked fainting as a sign of weakness.

The rules of town meetings were straightforward enough: Everyone got to speak. The rules of human nature were just as immutable: Everyone did speak, even though no one had anything to contribute that varied particularly from what the preceding orators had to offer except in quality of dramatic presentation. As a competition, it did not offer the cardiovascular benefits of bowling, but was just as enjoyable. Cheaper, too.

"I think it's wicked obvious." Maggie Fleck tossed in her nickel's worth after more than three hours of redundancy. "Business sucks in Dovekey because we have a serial kill'ah in town!" There were some groans in response, which Maggie took as encouragement. She pulled a face of beatific enlightenment. "We don't even know when this chain of heinous crimes began. You know, Claire, your husband could have been the first in a killin' spree. I always thought Bob's death was suspicious, and Asa and me was first on the scene."

Claire slowly rose from her seat in the front row, next to Frank.

"Pardon me, Maggie, but Bob passed away—in my humble opinion—as a direct result of too many town meetings held in the heat of the summer, to discuss how much money Dovekey Beach was not making for God-knows-what reason. The only thing you ought to be suspicious of, Maggie," Claire made eye contact, "is why I made by-God sure Bob was dead before I called you and Asa in for help."

Frank led the hoots and cheers in the high-ceilinged hall. His butt and the folding chair he was sitting in were having a serious disagreement. Ultimately, his butt had fallen asleep to avoid the conflict. Frank and all of his body parts were ready to go home, but it was not to be.

Rollie Ouimet rose for his moment in the spotlight.

"I bin tinkin' maybe you, dehr, shoudt tink about some recruitin', dehr, for de paramedic team. Maybe it's de fear of gettin' sick dat's keepin' de tourists away. Eh?"

Asa lost no time in deflecting criticism away from himself and his wife. He gave Rollie a roundhouse whack up the side of the skinny man's head. Terri Theresa Ouimet, loyal and true, kneed Asa in the groin.

Nothing like hands-on self-government, Frank thought.

The town selectmen and woman settled back in their chairs on the stage and waited for those nearest the hostility to subdue their peer group.

Ginny Philbrick might have found the discussion sufficiently over the top to have intervened, but she had left after an hour or so to have coffee with Ben Ryan. They had some talking to do about autopsies, lab reports, and coincidences.

Sometimes there can be far too much talking at and not enough listening to.

Some might say that there was enough guilt to go around. That is, had anyone been listening.

★   ★   ★

The *Curmudgeon* skated over the calm sea, navigating by the light of the stars and toward the illuminated steeple of the Congregationalist church in the center of town. Once closer to shore, Elizabeth would steer by the seat of her pants. The old lobster boat was designed for day work and had only running lights to keep her from being struck by more technologically gifted craft.

Without Frank on board, the trip was wonderfully restful. Elizabeth hummed tunelessly to herself. She even enjoyed rowing the heavy wooden dory from the mooring to the dock—the only job that was formally assigned to her father.

She began to consider MacKay's opinion that the stress of living under the same roof with Frank was making her overreactive. She did not consider MacKay's recommendation regarding Prozac.

As ugly as Frank's truck was, it ran a damn sight better than Elizabeth's MG. She was on a roll. The house was dark when she arrived just after 11:30. At that moment, Frank could have been with Claire in Las Vegas standing in front of an Elvis impersonator and entering into a bigamous marriage for all she cared. She could almost hear the deep claw-footed bathtub calling her name.

The back door was unlocked, as usual. Her mother, Sal, had tried to get the family to be more security conscious, but everyone except Sal kept losing the house keys. That was probably Elizabeth's mother's first step on the road to giving up: no keys. Anyway, as her father would say, that's why God made nature's burglar-alarm system, Petunia, the I-wonder-dog.

"Petunia, your sister is home!"

Elizabeth flipped on the light by the back door for her father, whenever he chose to return. She did not want to have to nurse him back to health if he tripped and broke a leg.

From years of practice, she bumped along in the dark to the forty-watt fixture over the kitchen table and turned it two clicks for just enough light to get to the stairway up and her longed-for bath. Her skin felt crusty from the hours in the salty air.

So much for perfect clarity.

The table was strewn with the remains of Frank's burrito-and-lobster-stew dinner, except for the broken glass and plate that had landed on the floor.

"You *better* hide, Petunia!"

Elizabeth counted her lucky star (she had only one, and knew it) that she had not cut herself to ribbons in the shadowy kitchen.

There was no puppy blood in the mess, nor did she expect any. The stupid dog cleared the table of dishes regularly. At the first explosion of shattered dishes, Petunia grabbed whatever munchies she had her eye on and disappeared under the bed in Frank's room to chow down at her leisure. Elizabeth knew she would not come out until Frank came home to protect her miserable hide.

He was always convinced that the two of them could talk it out, man-to-mutt.

"Damned cur!" Elizabeth complained to the broom closet. "Spoiled, that's what she is. Spoiled rotten," she made her case to the dustpan. "You're nothing more than a coyote on welfare, Petunia," she yelled toward Frank and Petunia's inner sanctum.

The broom bristles dragged on the gummy linoleum.

"What did you get into, dog?" Elizabeth had washed and waxed the floor recently in honor of Martha's and Eamon's arrival. She swept all the shards she could see into the dustpan, and wrote a quick note to Frank, warning him not to walk around barefooted until she had a chance to clean up in the daylight, and taped it to the back door.

If Elizabeth had wanted a soothing bubble bath before, she craved one now. Her fingers were sticking together and picking up lint from her own clothing. She turned on the hall light with her elbow, rather than leave fingerprints everywhere. Pink ones, she could see by the brighter light of the three-bulb ceiling lamp. She turned toward Frank's bedroom.

"If you got into my secret stash of red-hots, shit-for-brains, you are one dead dog," she informed the hiding Petunia—and tripped over the furry black body at the foot of the stairs.

"Oh, no!" She dropped to her knees next to the immobile cocker spaniel. "Oh, no." She lay her hand on the dog's side. It moved up and down steadily. Petunia was still alive, but barely.

"What did you do to yourself?" Elizabeth reached under the velvety muzzle, looking for a clue to what had felled Frank's favorite child.

"You better not have eaten any glass, you dummy." There were no cuts or blood on the spaniel's mouth, but the tongue lolled frighteningly extended in a frame of nasty foam and a puddle of vomit.

"Okay, Petunia. Okay. I take it all back. Just open your eyes, sweetie. Come on, honey." The dog did not stir. "Want a cookie? Open your eyes, Tuny, and Sissy will give you a cookie."

There was no response. Elizabeth checked again to be certain the dog was still breathing. Respiration had become shallower in just those few moments. Petunia's eyes were cloudy beneath their closed lids.

Elizabeth pushed both hands, palms up, under the flaccid dog's hips and shoulders and lifted Petunia to her chest. Using her buttocks as a battering ram, Elizabeth bumped open the back screen door and hightailed it for Frank's truck. She gently laid Petunia on the passenger side of the bench seat, and blessing the dear departed Mr. Chevrolet, gunned the engine and backed down the curving fifty-foot drive faster than would have been safe, hood-first.

Elizabeth calculated Dr. Sealy's office to be no more than seven minutes away, but this was the first time she would attempt the trip at fifty miles per hour, and without Petunia panting and dripping all over her lap, scrambling to stick her head out the driver's window.

It seemed longer, somehow.

The windows at the animal hospital were dark, as Elizabeth expected. Sean Sealy and his wife lived in the house set back behind the clinic. To Elizabeth's horror, the house, too, was as black as Petunia's coat. She threw herself at the door, yelling at the upstairs windows, anyway.

There was no one home.

Petunia was still unconscious in the truck. Her breathing had, impossibly, become even shallower. Tears ballooned in Elizabeth's eyes, and she irritably slapped her temples in order to see.

Elizabeth Will had only one place left to turn, and she knew she'd better turn there in time.

Otherwise, she might as well keep driving, all the way to Canada. Except, she reminded herself with a start, for all she knew, the only Canadian with whom she was more than casually acquainted might well be dead, himself, by now.

Elizabeth chided herself for being self-absorbed. She'd been brought up better than that, but she was beginning to take the whole situation in Dovekey Beach pretty darned personally.

NINE

ELIZABETH CRASHED BUTT-FIRST again through the back door. She was sweating so profusely, her fearful tears were lost in the perspiration shuffle. Terror had blown crimson into her face, and shortened her own breaths to tidy pants for air.

"Good Lord, Elizabeth! You like to give me a heart attack. Do you know what time—is that a dog?" Ben Ryan asked.

"I'm sorry, Doc," Elizabeth said, clutching her weakening bundle.

Ginny swung herself up from the kitchen table, knocking her mug of lukewarm coffee onto its side.

"Petunia," she called. "Petunia, baby, wake up." She stroked the animal's head softly, blowing into the dog's nose. No reaction.

Dr. Ryan was already at the door that led from his house to his examination room.

"This way, Elizabeth."

The two women followed the family doctor down the hall. He nodded to the examination table, and Elizabeth lay the dog down, still wrapped in the drop cloth she found in the back of the truck. Petunia's tongue had faded to an anemic shade of powder blue.

"What happened?" Doctor Ryan asked, plugging his stethoscope into his ears and placing the disk to the dog's chest. His blue-veined hands felt down her back and legs gently.

"I don't know, I don't know."

"Was she hit by a car, Biz?" Ginny asked. Funny, she thought. Her hands were shaking. After everything she had seen as a cop, the sight of this pathetic creature struggling for breath had gotten her sniffling. She allowed as how Frank's reaction if anything happened to his pride and joy might have something to do with it. For all his bluster, he was an A-number-one sucker when it came to animals, and Ginny would know. In addition to being Dovekey Beach's Top Cop, she was also the anointed animal-control officer—which included raccoons, otters, and chickadees. "Was it a car, Biz?" she repeated.

"No." Elizabeth pushed past Ginny to stroke Petunia's back. "No. I got home and she had pulled Dad's dinner off the table again. There was broken glass all over the place. I was afraid she may have swallowed some. You know how she just wolfs down her food."

"Good," Ryan said, "now, we have some place to start." He pried open Petunia's jaws and peered inside, using a penlight. "What did Frank have for dinner?"

"As far as I can tell, burritos and lobster stew."

"Why"—Dr. Ryan swished his fingers around the inside of Petunia's mouth—"knowing Frank's cholesterol count, does that not surprise me?" He wiped his right hand on a clean towel, opened a cabinet, and removed a length of tubing.

"Oh, my God!" Elizabeth breathed. "Dad wasn't home when I got there. What if the lobster stew went bad and he's in the hospital? I'd better call. May I?"

"Relax, Biz," Ginny reassured her. "I saw Frank at the

emergency town meeting an hour or so ago, and he was fine."

"Ginny," Ryan asked, "cut me a length of this tubing to about two feet, will you?" He turned to Elizabeth to explain while Ginny cut. "I'm taking a little chance here, but given the dog's condition, I don't think I can wait. Thanks, Ginny." He took the tube and started to feed it down Petunia's throat. "I'm not a veterinarian, but I know that if she swallowed glass, there's no saving her anyway. I'm guessing she got into some roadkill or a dead rodent."

"Not Petunia," Elizabeth disagreed. "She doesn't eat dog-things. Everything else, yes."

"Why didn't you take her to Sean?" Ginny asked.

"Not home. I tried."

The contents of Petunia's stomach started to empty through the tube and into a bedpan.

"That must be some town meeting," Ginny opined. "Sean and his wife were there, too. It must still be going on."

"Whatever," the doctor said. "Ginny, give Sealy's answering service a yell and tell them to get him over here as soon as possible. Tell them to let him know that the stomach contents are coming up pink."

"What does that mean?" Elizabeth asked, her heart thudding.

Ben Ryan patted the comatose spaniel lovingly.

"That I just may have made a whopper of an animal-husbandry faux pas."

Martha Robson hung over the white porcelain toilet, arms hugging the coolness of the bowl. With her stomach properly emptied, she felt much better. Nonetheless, she sat with amazing composure in her position on the ceramic tile floor.

By the patterning of white tile, with smaller black accents, Martha dated the bathroom from its original installation during the mid- to late-1920s. The large pedestal sink and claw-footed bathtub were consistent. Almost all the older homes in the village had at least one bath of that vintage. Her parents had two, and an older toilet with a box arrangement that flushed, compliments of gravity, next to the soapstone set tubs in the basement-cum-laundry room.

In northern Alberta, the plumbing was strictly modern, or absolutely outside. No 'twixt nor 'tween about it.

Martha laid her cheek against the tank. She missed her husband. Condensation ran down her cheek and puddled in the hollow of her neck.

When it comes to nausea, she thought, give me the good, old U S of A.

Ah, the comforts of home.

Petunia lay perfectly composed, eyes closed peacefully, in the small cubicle. Edith Ryan had provided the sparkling white towel beneath the small dog. The cotton terry had been hung outdoors on a clothesline, and still surrendered wisps of the crisply laundered smell. Elizabeth wished she could give the cocker a bath to bring back the puff and glossiness of her once-beautiful coat.

"You did the right thing, Liz," Dr. Sealy assured her. He rubbed her back, hoping she would bounce back. Everyone always expected the Wills to rebound. Elizabeth was looking bad this time, though. She probably should have stayed at Ryan's office, and let Sean do what he had to do. Naturally, she would not hear of it.

"Thanks, Sean."

"There's nothing you can do, now. Why don't you get yourself home and try to get some sleep?"

Ginny opened her eyes from where she had been dozing on her feet at the corner of the kennel.

"I'll follow her home in the cruiser, so she doesn't hit anything," she offered. Her beeper sprang to life. She tipped it up from her belt to read the numbers. "It's Doc Ryan." She pointed to the phone on the wall. "You mind?"

"Be my guest," Sean answered. Ginny dialed the old rotary telephone. To Elizabeth he said, "How that old man keeps these hours is beyond me. I'm ready to pack it in."

"Me, too," Elizabeth agreed. "But before I do, what am I going to tell my father?"

"Tell him we'll know better after analysis of Petunia's stomach, but that it looks to me like hemlock poisoning. It's really pretty common this time of year with hunting dogs."

"Please, Sean. We're talking about Petunia."

"Like it or not, it's what she was bred to do. Lots of birds feed on hemlock berries. Doesn't hurt them, but it poisons the meat. By the way, cursory blood work showed an elevated sugar level."

"Diabetes?"

"It's possible."

Ginny hung up the phone and called to Elizabeth.

"Okay, Biz. No rest for the wicked. Your father called the hospital when he got home to a wrecked house, and you were missing. Then he called the station, who referred him to Ben, who filled him in."

"Good. I don't have the energy."

"Well, you'd better find some. Frank's at the hospital waiting for us." Ginny did not wait for Elizabeth's next question. "Frank is fine, but Rose Sykes brought Martha into the emergency room about an hour and a half ago. She's had some kind of breakdown. Ben has been with her, so he hasn't had a chance to call Edith to let us know, until now."

Elizabeth balanced her head in her hands, elbows propped on the examination table.

"Just when you thought it was safe to walk down Memory

Lane. I don't think I can cope. Sean, when can I take the bot-tomless pit bull home with me?"

"Petunia should be all right by this afternoon, but I'd like to keep her overnight to keep an eye on her insulin."

"Be my guest, Sean. Ginny, you go on ahead. I have to get out of these clothes before they jump off me. I ought to give Avis a call, too. I'll be at the hospital in half an hour, forty-five min-utes, tops."

Sean Sealy walked the two women out of the kennel room, locking up behind himself. His assistant was due for work in less than thirty minutes. He shook out the tension in his shoulders.

"Good luck," he called after the retreating truck and car. He thought they were all due for some.

So did Elizabeth.

She more aimed than drove the rattling truck down Ocean Drive to connect up with the beach road. It was longer than tak-ing Route One, but safer for the other drivers out innocently tooling around on the same road with her in her dangerously sleep-deprived condition.

Rounding the corner, headed north past the Wild Rose Bed-and-Breakfast, Elizabeth caught a scent on the breeze. Numbly, she felt around in the Chevy's cold ashtray. Brilliant, she criticized herself. Better have a cup of coffee in the shower.

She sniffed the air again, and caught herself veering over the emphatically yellow line in the direction of Miss Locke's house. She blinked, and then blinked again for good measure.

A tower of black smoke rose from behind the back turret of the Victorian mansion.

Elizabeth cut off an unsuspecting sea-peeper in a shiny black Lincoln Town Car when she made a last-minute suicide swing into the bed-and-breakfast's drive.

The foyer was deserted and smelled faintly of potpourri. Elizabeth raced through the dining room and into the outdated kitchen. A large bowl of newly boiled shrimp chilled on ice to decorate breakfast plates. A tasteful touch.

"Miss Locke?" She sniffed again. The smell of smoke was back, but the air was clear inside the house. She slammed out the kitchen door and through the herb garden to get a better view of the back of the house and the second floor. As she careered around the corner, narrowly missing a harrowing fall into the open bulkhead, she came upon the source of the fire.

"Why, Elizabeth!" Miss Locke said, one hand placed on her chest in surprise. "I would have thought you would be at the hospital. You did get word, didn't you?"

Elizabeth collapsed on the lawn, crushing several previously hardy violets, and laughed.

"I thought the Wild Rose was on fire." She laughed another good one at herself. "This week, a splashy conflagration would have just figured."

"Yes, dear, you're right about that." Miss Locke threw a basket of dried leaves onto the top of the fire she had made in the barbecue stand her father had built himself out of native rock. Elizabeth recoiled at the scent of melting plastic.

"Miss Locke? I know it's none of my business, but why are you building a fire in the backyard at"—she looked at her wristwatch—"six-thirty-five in the morning?"

Miss Locke appeared positively abashed.

"Well, dear, I know it's against the town ordinance, but since we all have to pay for trash removal, Rose and I have been sort of sneaking a little of our rubbish out here for disposal." She waited politely for Elizabeth to stop laughing. "Now of course we compost our green garbage, and Rose is very fastidious about not burning petroleum-based products. They're carcinogenic, you know."

"I know," Elizabeth said, remembering to dig in her pockets for a pack of carcinogens and matches. They'd fallen out somewhere during the long, long, night. Her best guess was out on Piscatawk with MacKay. She blushed and stood, feeling foolish and very, very tired. The strange odor was overwhelmed by the crackling leaves.

"Are you all right, Elizabeth? You're looking rather pale, dear."

"Just my normal color, Miss Locke. I'm fine."

"And Petunia?"

As noted, word does travel fast.

"Dr. Sealy thinks she got into some game that had been feeding on hemlock berries. She couldn't get enough oxygen. I don't know, though."

"Now, Elizabeth, you should keep your mind open regarding these medical matters. Why, in the old days, during the Depression, there were lots of accidental poisonings. People were hungry. They went foraging and didn't know what they were harvesting. Oh, my!" Miss Locke wrung her fragile hands. "Eamon was out picking berries for me before he got sick. You don't suppose?" She let the inference hang amidst morning birdsong.

Elizabeth immediately shook her head in the negative. "Miss Locke, you washed and served the berries. Remember? Surely you would have noticed any inedible fruit."

"That's true, that's true. But we don't know what Eamon might have nibbled on while he was out in the patch, do we? And hemlock is one of the most common wild bushes in the Northeast, you know."

"I didn't know that."

"Well, it is. I think you should mention it to Doctor Ryan. I definitely do." She stirred the fire with a long tong. Embers shot skyward like startled fireflies in the sun. Miss Locke looked tinier every day.

142

Time marches on, and sometimes it stomps the hell out of you.

"Are you and Mrs. Sykes doing all right?" Elizabeth asked. "I mean, I know it's none of my business, but you both seem to be working so hard, lately. I worry."

"Oh, dear," Miss Locke propped the fire tongs at the side of the barbecue. "Don't you worry about us. The inn here has had a little setback, but I have my small trade in preserves and a few piano lessons every week, and Rose has regular tutorial students to supplement her school pension. Making do is a true mark of strength."

"I'm not so sure about that, Miss Locke."

"Well, I am, dear. Sometimes doing without builds character. There is too much emphasis put on material goods, these days. And such attention is unseemly." She closed the subject.

Elizabeth wondered what Miss Locke would think if she knew that Elizabeth lulled herself to sleep nine nights out of ten with visions of material goods dancing in her head.

The tenth night was usually wasted on running a list of why she would never succeed in the pursuit of the upper middle class.

Miss Locke would find that pessimistic.

And pessimism, along with avarice, was considered unladylike in the extreme. But, then, so was extremism.

Whoever was responsible for the deaths in Dovekey must not have cared. Live Free or Die.

What a state motto.

"Haven't seen a case of hemlock poisoning since the Depression," Dr. Ryan dismissed the idea. "Except in a couple of stupid dogs, naturally. Mostly Irish setters, though I couldn't tell you why."

"Miss Locke said that I should keep my mind open regarding these matters," Elizabeth defended herself, and retargeted the subject at hand.

"Well, then," Frank admonished them both. "Fact is, Eamon told me himself that he was a farm boy. There's not a berry in those woods that'd kill ya' that looks anything t'all like a blackberry. Give the boy some credit for the brains God gave a raccoon."

"Eamon's condition has stabilized," Dr. Ryan said. "I wish I knew if I did anything to promote it. Right now, I'm more concerned about Martha."

"May I see her?" Elizabeth asked.

"You can take a quick peek, but as for a visit, I'm 'fraid not, Lizzie. She took one look at Eamon and just collapsed. I had her admitted, and when she wakes up, I'm going to sedate her all over again."

"She's all right, isn't she? Doc, tell me she's not going to end up plugged into some machine next to Eamon in there."

"Now, calm down, Lizzie. Considering everything, she appears to be healthy enough. She's hanging by her fingernails over the edge of one of her spells again, and, don't you worry; this time I'm not going to let her drop."

"Wait a minute." Elizabeth grasped the doctor's wrist to keep him from squirming out of the conversation. "Are you telling me that Martha is having a nervous breakdown?"

"Call it what you will, Liz. Martha needs a good long rest. I don't think coming back here was the best idea for her right now."

"Right now?" Elizabeth repeated. "What about fourteen years ago?" She did not release her hold on the old man. "Are you trying to tell me that one of my best friends in the world had a nervous collapse right under my nose and I didn't know it? How could that be?"

"You were only seventeen, Elizabeth," Frank said as though that could explain anything, and uncurled her fingers from the doctor's arm. "Kids today understand too damned much, if you ask me. There was nothing you could do to help, ya' know."

"Well, I *don't* know. Someone should have asked, before squirreling her away like some psychotic second cousin." Elizabeth clutched her stomach, a nameless shame roiling from a fourteen-year-old place deep in her gut. No one talked about the Drakes after their dash to the nether regions of Canada. Not after a while, anyway.

Every time Elizabeth or Avis brought up the subject, their mother shut them down as quick as a toxic waste dump. After a while, they stopped asking.

Come the fall, Ginny and Elizabeth went off to college without the Third Musketeer. Once or twice a year, one or both of them would dash off an inane teenage note to Martha without giving it more than a second thought.

"Was she committed to a sanitarium, or did the Drakes just pull the shades and wait for Martha to get over it?" Elizabeth demanded. "I don't know why they thought they had to move to another country. Why, I know for a fact that the Drakes had a 'mad room' on the top floor." An amazing number of nineteenth-century homes did—dark, airless cells where members of the family who had become dangerous to themselves or others, or were simply too embarrassing to let out in the daylight were stored like preserves in a pantry. "Must run in the family, huh? No big deal."

"It wasn't like that, Lizzie," Ben Ryan said. He looked to Frank for support. Frank nodded. "Martha Drake was high-strung, for sure. But she was also pregnant. That's why her parents up and moved. They wouldn't give consent for her to marry, and she wouldn't terminate the pregnancy. Martha was so overwrought, I had to agree. They did what they thought was best. This is a very small town, Liz."

Elizabeth shook her head.

"Unbelievably small."

"People are entitled to their secrets, Lizzie," said Ryan.

"Some secret," Elizabeth grumbled. "Seems like I'm the only one who didn't know it."

"Come on, Lizzie." Frank took his daughter's arm. "Let's go home. Too late to take the boat out, and the lobsters'll be happy enough to wait for us till tomorrow."

As much as Elizabeth would have liked to curl up into a fetal position, a Mercedes pulled into one of the gallery parking spots just ahead of Elizabeth and Frank's arrival.

Rather than rattle around the dogless house, both of the Wills chose to remain down the hill.

It took almost an hour to negotiate, but Elizabeth ultimately sold the New York couple six small matted watercolor renderings of various wildflowers, and a major custom-framed landscape: the best in the shop.

To the couple's surprise, Elizabeth accepted their personal check. She had never gotten a rubber one, but Frank would chew her out good and proper for her leap of faith.

She went outside to show off how substantial the amount was, and allow him to get his lecture over with.

Frank was scraping his precious bumper sticker off the back of his truck. It was a small gesture, but duly noted. The faded "Is your church ATF approved?" missive was still stuck next to the shredded residue. Elizabeth appreciated her father's attempt at supportiveness, but not enough to let him off the hook.

"Did Avis know?" she asked, going back to the subject of Martha's illegitimate pregnancy. An hour had given her the luxury of fully processing the information—in light of the times and the town.

"Of course not. She was only fou'ahteen." Frank plucked stray paper from the gummy smear. "And before you ask, far as I know, neither did Ginny. And if it makes you feel any bettah, neither did I. It was one of those Ladies' Guild things, I guess."

"Then why didn't Mother tell me?"

"Guess she figured t'wasn't any a' your business. T'wasn't either."

"You people are amazing."

"Your moth'ah figured t'ain't catchin'."

"Oh," Elizabeth disagreed, "I think she did."

And if there was one thing Elizabeth Will had worked out in her mind, it was that one thing surely led to another. The past week had proved it.

But what was that first thing that set the rest of the dominoes of death tumbling?

And what would be the last?

TEN

THE MOON HAD started waning, but still hovered, spewing ghostly incandescence over the coastline. "Closed beach" signs, broken and stuffed into aluminum-mesh trash cans waited patiently for morning removal. A block of light cut on and off in less time than it took to recognize it as coming from the opening of a car door beyond the seawall.

The figure moved slowly, but navigated the granite boulders with practiced dexterity. It moved more quickly to the low-tide mark, trousered legs lashing in military fashion. A yard back from the lapping water, the figure turned back toward the road and three-hundred-car parking lot.

An arm swung gracefully away from the dark clot of clothing, as though to anoint the sand surrounding it. Ritualistically, it mobilized: Five steps and a blessing, five steps and a blessing.

The ceremony ceased with the figure's disappearance into the craggy tumble at the base on the incline.

Had anyone seen it, they would have thought the rite somehow beautiful.

★ ★ ★

Asa and Maggie Fleck shot in and out of the crowd doing a frantic imitation of competence. Vinnie sweated bullets and whacked flesh off a massive leg bone and onto luau-sized trays. Claire Wallis handed the carnage through a hole in the wall to Frank for him to align on the paper-covered tables.

"More brown bread?" MacKay asked Elizabeth.

"You're such a sport, MacKay," she answered.

"I thought a Daughter of the American Revolution would find a ham-and-bean supper inspirational and uplifting."

"Well, *this* Daughter of the American Revolution did not expect a dinner invitation, last–minute as it may have been, to have involved an evening in the Congregational Church basement." Elizabeth took a slice of the molasses-laden brown bread and placed it on the side of her soggy paper plate. "Call me high-maintenance."

"Just like her mother," Frank pronounced, and planted himself in the tan folding chair to MacKay's right. His plate was piled inches deep with food. The paper folded on impact with the table, leaving a watery trail of bean juice and coleslaw mayonnaise.

"No, suh," Avis chimed in from Elizabeth's right.

"Thank you," said Elizabeth.

"You're welcome," Avis said. "I'm glad you like the brown bread. I was up all night steaming it." Maggie's arm darted between Elizabeth and her sister to dump a refill into the aluminum bowl.

"Thank you for supporting the Dovekey Beach Paramedic Emergency Squad," she parroted for the tenth time and made a return dash to the kitchen.

"What brings you to dry land, MacKay?" Frank asked through a mouthful of baked ham.

"Guest lecture at the Portsmouth Adult Education Center.

That and the beans." Elizabeth gave her date a withering glance that was completely wasted on him. "I also wanted to take a look at Eamon."

"And?" Elizabeth urged.

"And have a talk with Dr. Ryan," MacKay conceded. "Boy, they give you a lot of food at these things."

"The Ladies' Guild was expecting a larger turnout," Avis explained.

"Spineless tourists no doubt feared eating the native dishes without their own stomach pumps," commented Elizabeth. "Asa and Maggie don't go very far in assuaging such health concerns."

"Now, Biz," Avis warned. "Asa and Maggie have been working very hard. We all have. It's not like we're not all working overtime, lately, to compensate."

"This morning I caught Miss Locke burning trash to save a few bucks. She's too old to have to do that." Elizabeth had been dwelling on the sad picture throughout the day. She admitted it might have been to keep her mind off the Robsons, for a change. Even so, the memory had disquieted her. Especially the fact that Miss Locke had lied about what she was incinerating.

Avis was thrown for a minute by her sister's genuine concern. "She's working like a twenty-year-old in the kitchen right now," she countered. "She's much stronger than she looks."

"She'd have to be." Frank left the folding table to return to his duties. And Claire Wallis, Elizabeth reckoned.

"I haven't seen Mrs. Sykes."

"Oh." Avis cleared disintegrating paper from the table. "She had a student tonight, so she's watching the inn." Her sister leaped up to help.

"We should take her some leftovers."

"What?" MacKay asked.

"Elizabeth," said Avis, "I'm sure Miss Locke will bring a

plate home for Mrs. Sykes. Besides, I'm on the clean-up committee. I have responsibilities here."

"What about me?" asked MacKay.

"You're lecturing, MacKay. When are you due at the community center?"

He checked his watch. "Not for forty-five minutes."

"I'm sure you want to go over your teaching aids."

"E-liz-a-beth"—Avis drew out the name—"what are you up to?"

"Ditto," MacKay seconded.

"Let's go," Elizabeth bullied her sister. "I'll have you back in time for your precious cleanup. MacKay, I'll meet you at Rosa's for an after-dinner drink. Say, ten-thirty." Without waiting for agreement, Elizabeth pushed Avis ahead of her and out the door.

Avis had to push the MG to get it started, so Elizabeth explained herself on the road to the Wild Rose as a reward.

"I hate this," Avis complained in the claustrophobic bucket seat.

"You do not *hate* anything, Avis Arlene Donigian," Elizabeth recited, "you dislike it intensely."

"Sure. *Now* you get an attack of manners. Can I take it to mean you have changed your mind regarding your plan to stick your nose into places it doesn't belong? Searching another person's home is not only a vulgar invasion of privacy, Biz, it's illegal."

"So call a cop."

"That's not a bad idea." Avis was willing to grasp at any straw. "Let's talk to Ginny. Call me silly, but she can get a nice legal search warrant and leave me out of it."

"Silly," Elizabeth answered as directed. "In the first place, I don't know what I'm looking for. In the second place, Ginny told me to keep my nose out of other people's business."

"Wow!" Avis mumbled. "I *am* a goofball."

Elizabeth put the MG in first and turned off the engine. "Sarcasm does not become you."

"Too bad a suspicious nature suits *you*." Avis could not get her seat belt to release her and ended up crawling out from underneath the shoulder strap. "And when this is over, would you please buy a new car?"

Elizabeth pushed open the front door of the Wild Rose. Despite its solid oak construction, it swung open easily. Whatever guests the two elderly sisters may have had, the house was quiet. From the road, Elizabeth had seen only one room illuminated on the second floor. Perhaps Mrs. Sykes was already in bed.

"I'm really going to hate you if we wake her up," Avis threatened.

"Shush. I can hear something in the kitchen. I'll bet she's getting ready for tomorrow morning. Just help me tonight and I'll, uh, baby-sit for you sometime."

Avis followed her sister through the foyer and dining room in the direction of the kitchen. She could hear the sound then. It was a whirring unlike any baking sound with which she was familiar, and Avis was familiar with them all.

"What is that?" she asked.

"I don't know," Elizabeth whispered. The kitchen lights were all on, but the room was empty. "Refrigerator?" Avis shook her head. Elizabeth followed the continuous whir to one of the six doors—garden, pantry, servant's stairway, dining room, hall, and butler's pantry-cum-summer kitchen—that led off the main room and, in conjunction with the three windows cut between, made modern cabinetry installation impossible. "Mrs. Sykes," Elizabeth called at the summer-kitchen door from where the sound emanated. "Mrs. Sykes?" She placed her hand on the porcelain knob.

"I *hate* this," Avis complained once more for good measure.

Elizabeth opened the door. Mrs. Sykes looked up from a textbook curiously.

"Why girls, is there something wrong?" She stood up from her stool. "Has anything happened to Amelia?"

"Oh, no, Mrs. Sykes. Miss Locke is fine," Elizabeth stammered a bit. "Avis and I thought that with her at the bean supper, you might need some help here. Or maybe some company."

Chalking up the show of consideration to the younger of the Will sisters, Mrs. Sykes smiled at Avis. "How very sweet of you. As a matter of fact, my student has left, and I was just wondering how I was going to amuse myself until Amelia got home. Why don't I make us all some nice tea?"

"Thank you," Avis answered. "That would be lovely."

Lovely, Elizabeth thought. No wonder everyone mistook Avis for the nice one. Lovely, indeed. Truly a Mary Poppins adjective.

"What a shame you missed Claire earlier," Mrs. Sykes reported. "She dropped by to report on how the Robsons are doing. Tragic."

"Tragic," Elizabeth agreed. "Mrs. Sykes, may I use the powder room?"

"Why, of course, Elizabeth. You know where it is. There are guest towels on the top of the commode, as always. Avis and I will put together a snack."

"Thank you."

"You're welcome, Elizabeth. Now, Avis," Mrs. Sykes flicked off the switch to the circular machinery making the noise, "why don't we find that gilded camel teapot you were always so fond of when you were a child?"

Elizabeth wondered why it would not occur to Mrs. Sykes to dust off the royal blue and mustard yellow goose teapot that was her favorite, but opted to exit rather than whine. She had hauled her sister away from the church basement for more than a scone and a ceramic pot that puked tea through its mouth.

The Wild Rose did not have a lavatory on the first floor. For seven years apiece, both of the Will sisters had taken piano lessons in the house when it had been only that. Elizabeth first, Avis second, just as they had come into the world. Out of sheer boredom, during Avis's half-hour, Elizabeth had logged many hours in the big bathroom that smelled wonderfully of Lady Esther face powder, reading *Reader's Digest* magazines and doing some childish snooping in the medicine cabinet.

She took the main staircase two treads at a time. She carried her fancy "date" sandals in her hand for the sake of quiet and safety. Huffing just a little, she reached the door to the Robsons' room and prayed that it be unlocked.

Of course it was.

For the life of her, she did not know what she was looking for, or what she planned to do with anything she found. It had been so easy for her to accept that Martha was, as they say in polite society, unbalanced. She felt disloyal about that.

The truth was, she and Ginny had never talked about it (naturally), but both of them had always been easier on Martha than they had been on each other. It may have been instinct. If it was, it was the same instinct that dogs have when they are assailed by small children: a natural understanding that the child is weaker and smaller than they.

The Robsons' private bath yielded nothing of interest. The suitcases had all been unpacked, the clothing folded neatly in the bureau. As quickly as she could, Elizabeth fingered through each drawer. Shorts, lingerie, blue jeans, just laundry. She was on the verge of relief and nearly out the door when, on a whim, she pulled open the top drawer of the small table next to the bed.

Though she wanted to return to the kitchen before she was

missed, Elizabeth could not resist opening both Eamon's and Martha's passports. She was a bit deflated to find that Martha looked marvelous, even in her passport photo. It was Eamon who looked like the psycho. Beneath the passports was Eamon's National Health card, and some other official-looking papers.

Elizabeth lay the documentation in her hand on the table-top for a closer look at what was beneath. The papers were United States issue.

To her amazement, she had found something valuable.

Elizabeth swept everything back in the drawer and, feeling the utter and complete fool, closed the door silently behind herself.

Fortunately, she had made note of her trail on this trip to Martha's bedroom and did not lose herself. She made it to Miss Locke's bathroom in record time, flushed the toilet quickly, lightly mussed a guest towel, and hurried back to Avis and Mrs. Sykes.

Again, the kitchen was empty. The door to the butler's panty was ajar and dimly lit by a decorative night-light. All was still. She wondered where Avis had gotten herself to, when she noticed a silvery label affixed to the side of what looked to be an electric canning cooker. It read: PROPERTY OF DOVEKEY BEACH SCHOOL. Pilfering school supplies seemed out of character for Mrs. Sykes. She must have borrowed it for one of her students' experiments.

Elizabeth glanced over her shoulder for signs of life. Reassured that she was alone, she squeezed through the unlatched paneled door for a closer look.

Strange.

Opposite the work station, the deep porcelain sink sparkled. Damp paper towels covered the crushed powder of what Elizabeth assumed to be a broken chemistry vessel. She refocused.

The stainless-steel cylinder opened effortlessly. Hanging

from a central fixture were three test tubes, each one stoppered. She lifted one from its cradle, and took it into the brighter kitchen for examination when she heard a voice coming toward the kitchen door.

Feeling like a cat with canary feathers hanging out of her mouth, she dropped the vial into the purse Avis had left on the table in the center of the room.

"Why, Elizabeth, there you are," Mrs. Sykes said. "Can you believe, I've become so doddering I forgot the sugar." She lifted a baby camel with a lid on its back from the glass-fronted china cupboard and poured sugar from the utilitarian model next to the loaded purse into it. "Come along, Elizabeth. Your sister and I decided to move to the parlor for our tea."

Elizabeth swung the pocketbook strap over her shoulder and followed Mrs. Sykes back through the dining room and foyer, into the formal parlor.

It seemed an eternity before Avis begged their leave to return to help with the cleanup at the church. Elizabeth strapped Avis' pocketbook on to her herself, and carried the tea tray back to the sink for Mrs. Sykes.

Outside, Avis commented, "That was oddly tidy of you, Biz."

"Give me your purse. You drive, I'll push."

"You're not making any sense, Biz."

"You think I don't *know* that? Now, get behind the wheel and pop the clutch when I yell."

Elizabeth threw herself in the open passenger door as soon as the engine caught.

"Well?" Avis asked.

"I was wrong," Elizabeth answered quickly before the words caught in her throat. "Martha may have her problems, but I found proof that she would prefer her husband alive."

"I hope you're ashamed of yourself."

"A little."

"How did you convince your paranoid self?" Avis asked.

"A United States resident-alien application tucked in with their passports. Martha and Eamon are planning to move back."

Avis set her mouth in a straight line. "Well," she repeated, "I hope you're ashamed of yourself."

Elizabeth promised herself never to confide in her sister ever, ever again.

Smoke veiled the polished wood, but it was darkness that made the people squint at one another. It made Elizabeth wonder what Rosa's Cara Mia Lounge was like on, say, date night and not a Thursday.

"C'mon MacKay," Elizabeth shouted over the music when she at last located him in the throng.

"I just got my drink!" he objected.

Elizabeth swallowed the shot of Irish whiskey and hid the bottle of Budweiser under her jacket. MacKay didn't catch up with her until she was standing next to the Eternal Sea van. The administrator of the nonprofit organization left it on the town dock for dry-dock emergencies, such as pivotal rugby matches against the Manchester team, ham-and-bean suppers, and murder investigations.

"I hope you paid the tab, MacKay." She handed him his beer. "Let's pay Doc Ryan a visit."

Edith Ryan answered Elizabeth's knock at the kitchen door.

"Ben's asleep, Elizabeth," Edith scolded. She pointedly glanced up at the clock on the wall. "I would have been upstairs myself by now, but we had a special bowling-league game tonight."

"Sorry," Elizabeth apologized. MacKay rolled his eyes backward in their sockets. "We don't need to wake him, if you could just let us into his office to use his microscope."

Edith Ryan resisted. "I think it might be better if you were to wait for the morning. Ben is up bright and early."

"Good idea, Mrs. Ryan," said MacKay.

"*Bad* idea, MacKay," Elizabeth argued. "As soon as my mind is set to rest, the sooner I'll stop annoying the hell out of you."

"Mrs. Ryan, please?" MacKay asked.

"The room is open," Edith answered, "but know upfront that that microscope is older than Ben."

"Thank you, Mrs. Ryan," Elizabeth said.

Edith nodded. "Now, I'll make the coffee, but you two be quiet, you hear? Ben needs his rest, and I'll be whipped if I end up a widow out of this mess."

"Thank you, Mrs. Ryan," said Elizabeth. Apparently, all the extra time spent lately with the Ladies' Guild was having a beneficial effect on her basic manners.

Elizabeth found her way easily into the doctor's office. She located the light switch with more difficulty.

"What are you doing?" MacKay asked as Elizabeth pulled sundry equipment from various drawers and cabinets.

"I am making up a specimen slide."

"Impressive, Will. What do you need me for?"

"To read it, you oaf." Elizabeth pulled the purloined vial from her jacket pocket and set it in a stand. After some rummaging, she found a box of clean slides and another of slide covers. MacKay observed, fascinated that Elizabeth seemed to know what she was doing. She caught him watching. "Premed," she explained, using an eyedropper to deposit a tiny amount of the contents of Mrs. Sykes's vial, and delicately covering the spot of liquid with the paper-thin glass cover.

The microscope was as Edith Ryan had described. Though fully forty years old, it did have a light, for which Elizabeth was grateful. She turned on the tiny bulb, and positioned the slide in place. After a few twists of the focus knobs, she stood back.

"Okay, MacKay. What have we got?"

Charles MacKay bent over the low microscope and placed his eye to the viewer.

"*Gonyaulax catenella,*" he answered. "Red-tide dinoflagellates. Where did you get this?"

"From a centrifuge."

"Obviously. That explains the high concentration." He lowered his eye for another look. "And who do you know who owns his own centrifuge?"

"Good question," Ben Ryan called from the doorway. He was dressed hastily in a snappy, plaid bathrobe and felt slippers.

"Coffee's served in the kitchen," Edith called from behind her husband. "Come on in. God only knows what disease you could catch drinking it in there."

ELEVEN

THE NIGHT NURSE dozed by Eamon Robson's bedside, a Barbara Taylor Bradford novel open on her lap. With the respirator and cardiac monitors turned off, the intensive care unit was as quiet as a chapel.

Eamon's pale face was briefly lit from the corridor lights sneaking entry through the crack of the slowly closing door.

"Call Ginny," MacKay ordered.

"I can't," Elizabeth said. "I'm supposed to be keeping my nose out of her investigation."

"What a concept," MacKay commented.

Ben Ryan sighed. "And Ginny was right, Elizabeth. It's time for you to get your bloomers untwisted. It just so happens that Eamon Robson regained consciousness not three short hours ago. He is going to recover, Lizzie. As far as I can tell, he suffered little or no brain damage. Now that he's awake, I can do some more tests tomorrow. In the daylight," he emphasized.

"Really?" Elizabeth's eyes filled with tears of fatigue and relief, MacKay noted sourly. "Thank God."

"Really," Ryan reassured her. "Hence, my foolish decision to go to bed and get some sleep. Morning rounds come early enough."

"Let's go," MacKay moaned. "I'll call Ginny myself as soon as it's decent; you're going to bed."

"No, MacKay! Not until we catch the person who did this to Eamon. How can you deny the truth when I stick it right under your bloodshot eyeball?"

"That does it," MacKay walked to the wall phone. "I'm calling Ginny right now."

"For God's sake," Ben Ryan interrupted, "let the poor woman sleep. Someone in this town ought to get a full eight hours of shut-eye." He paused to refill his coffee cup. "We really don't have any proof of anything here, except that a science teacher is doing some science on the side to earn a few extra dollars. Dr. MacKay here does the same thing every day, and I don't see anyone accusing him of attempted murder. To think Rose Sykes capable of poisoning an entire population is jumping the gun, to say the least."

"I wasn't," Elizabeth protested.

"Sounded that way to me," MacKay argued. "Look, the feds are all over this thing. I am all over this thing. The clam flats are safe. Dr. Ryan agrees that Eamon Robson's symptoms were too severe to be caused by seafood paralytic poisoning alone when the concentrations are at such a low level."

"He has no built-up immunity. He's a northern Canadian, for God's sake. It wouldn't take that much. Besides, as we just proved, it doesn't take a rocket scientist to concentrate a lethal dose of those cellular monsters," Elizabeth said stubbornly.

"Eamon could *not* have ingested enough, Elizabeth." MacKay dug in his heels. "Unless the murderer was following him from meal to meal. He was complaining about feeling under the weather for a few days before he convulsed."

"That's right," Ryan agreed.

"Unless," Elizabeth reasoned, "someone spiked his food with a dinoflagellate concentrate. Bang! One fell swoop."

"And you think Rose Sykes slipped it into his eggs? How could she do that without poisoning everyone—or, hell, just *one* other guest—at the inn?" MacKay got up to pace. "Believe me, he'd taste it in his coffee or most anything else."

Elizabeth glared at MacKay. "I told you, I don't think Mrs. Sykes did any such thing. I think she's covering for someone else. Mrs. Ryan," she called to Ben's wife, now watching television in the living room beyond, "do you still have that drop cloth I used on Petunia?"

Edith stuck her face in the kitchen.

"The what?"

"The drop cloth, Mrs. Ryan. Do you still have it?"

"Yes, Elizabeth. It's in the laundry room. I was going to wash it up for you. It still has some use left in it. No shame in making do."

"Right!" Elizabeth jumped from her chair. "This way?" she asked Mrs. Ryan as she dashed past muttering, "Use it up, wear it out, make it do." She came back with an armful of dirty sheeting. "Let's take a look at this under the lens, shall we?" She led the way back into the examination room.

MacKay watched Elizabeth tear a strip from the sheet. "*Now* who do you think is our crazed terrorist?"

She positioned the small square of material in the microscope and turned on the light. She stood back to allow both men a peek.

"Miss Locke," she pronounced without pleasure. The men stared at her as though wondering where to find a straitjacket at such an hour of the night. "Go ahead," she gestured to the microscope. "Take a look. Tell me, what do you see?"

162

MacKay and Dr. Ryan took turns peering into the eyepiece. Elizabeth waited patiently.

"I see dog barf," MacKay said at last. "Specifically, *pink* dog barf." Ben Ryan looked skyward for divine guidance.

"I'd have to agree," affirmed the doctor.

Elizabeth barged her way between the two men for her own double-check.

"No dinoflagellates?"

The men shook their heads.

"None?"

"Not a one," Dr. Ryan answered.

Elizabeth collapsed onto the examination stool. "I was so sure. Petunia's symptoms mirrored Eamon's in so many ways. Then it hit me: high blood sugar, sticky mess. Petunia scarfed down a jar of Miss Locke's rose-hip jelly."

"And heaven knows what else," said Dr. Ryan. "That dog is a canine trash can. Ask Sean Sealy tomorrow if the high sugar could have thrown her into coma," he advised, knowing it was probable.

"You need sleep, Liz," MacKay prodded. "You're grasping at straws. My guess is you'll feel better once you visit with Eamon."

"And what is that supposed to mean?" Elizabeth said.

"Lizzie, Dr. MacKay is just trying to say that he thinks your affection for your friends has made you lose sight of the bigger picture."

"Like what?"

"Oh, rattlesnakes, ship fires, medical waste, shark sightings. That stuff," MacKay summarized. "That'd keep a little old lady pretty busy, now wouldn't it?"

Edith snickered from the doorway.

"I do apologize, Elizabeth," she offered, "it's just that I had this vision of Amelia Locke smuggling a great white shark in that foolish tapestry knitting bag of hers."

Ginny turned on the flashing blue lights of the cruiser, as much to see as to break up the party on the beach. It was not that the chief of police had become a party pooper in her old age, but the beach was closed after midnight. Blame the town ordinance designed to cut down on the number of teenage beer bashes she was about to disperse.

Ginny knew that three-quarters of the revelers would escape to the smelly haven of the salt marsh before she could corral them, but that was punishment enough in her estimation. She and Elizabeth had done their time during high school, slammed facedown in the greasy mush to save themselves from a good talking-to from the police.

To Ginny Philbrick's shock, rather than make a run for it, the party came to her.

The inebriated kids were slow and unsteady, but they were definitely making the chase a whole lot easier than usual. The chief caught sight of the leaders in the glare of her high-powered flashlight.

Blood ran from the youngsters' legs, feet, and hands. Several of the kids dropped to the parking-lot pavement the moment they reached it. Ginny got on the horn to the dispatcher, waking her out of a sound sleep.

"Get the paramedics down to the state beach, pronto," she ordered. "Better call the Pebble Beach rescue team down here, too."

"It's not like you to give in so easily," MacKay commented, taking a slow turn down the beach road.

"I am bowed, but not beaten," Elizabeth quoted. "Take a left here, please."

Too tired to react quickly, MacKay did as he was told, and pulled into the driveway of the Wild Rose Bed-and-Breakfast. He stopped the van twenty feet from the door.

"It's a little bit late in the evening to be making apologies to Miss Locke, Elizabeth," he lectured and put the vehicle in reverse. Elizabeth opened the passenger door and stepped out before he released the brake.

"Yes, it is," Elizabeth agreed. She started to walk up the drive to the front door. MacKay threw the car in park, turned off the motor, and followed her.

"Elizabeth," he whispered, "get a *grip,* will you? It's the middle of the night. You wake up those old ladies and you'll give them both a heart attack."

"I won't be waking them." Elizabeth pointed to the cars parked off to the side, behind the wild-rose hedge. See? They're entertaining." She marched deliberately around to the kitchen door, knocked twice, and let herself in. The screen door slammed in MacKay's face.

"Elizabeth!" Claire Wallis exclaimed.

The heart and soul of the Dovekey Ladies' Guild observed Elizabeth Will wide-eyed from the kitchen table.

"Would you like some tea, dear?" Miss Locke asked from her position behind the teapot. It was Elizabeth's favorite: the brightly colored goose.

"Thank you, Miss Locke. That would be lovely." Elizabeth took a chair and laid a napkin in her lap.

"Would your friend like a cup?" Miss Locke nodded to the shadow of Charles MacKay outside and poured, as Claire Wallis and Rose Sykes looked on. MacKay entered the room sheepishly and took a place at the table.

All the while, MacKay pondered what a field day an abnormal-psychology professor would have poking around here.

He shuddered at the unbidden bastardization of the academics' credo: 'Publish *and* perish.'

Elizabeth handed a delicate porcelain cup of tea to MacKay, and then took one for herself. She took a sip before speaking.

"Thank you."

"You're welcome, Elizabeth," Miss Locke answered. "Now, may I inquire as to the purpose of your visit?"

"I'm curious," Elizabeth answered.

Despite his best intentions, MacKay sniffed his tea suspiciously.

"How can we help?" Mrs. Sykes asked.

"I'd like to know why the esteemed Ladies' Guild of Dovekey Beach is killing tourists this season."

MacKay dropped his cup. The thin china exploded on the kitchen floor.

The chief of police rousted her roommate, Sandy, out of bed, half because she needed another pair of hands to post the "Beach Closed" signs, and half because Ginny was sick and tired of suffering alone.

Between Asa and Maggie's ambulance, the Pebble Beach ambulette, and Mr. Elwell's station wagon, all eleven of the cut teenagers had transportation to the regional emergency room.

Asa and Maggie Fleck earnestly discussed field amputations at some length, but Ginny judged that only five of the injured really required so much as stitches and forbid any in-transit interventions.

Someone had gone to a lot of trouble to grind the glass that was strewn over the beach into troublesome near-powder consistency. How considerate, the Chief thought.

Premeditated, too.

Damn the town budget! It would just about kill her, but it was looking like she might have to go begging to Dick Dawley to commandeer a couple of his summer cops until she could convince the selectmen to let her hire her own rent-a-cops.

Ginny Philbrick almost wished that she had allowed Elizabeth to help her out. There was not a nosier person in Rockingham County, except maybe Frank, and both of them had a nasty tendency to fly by the seat of their pants.

And then she remembered another.

Mayor Dick Dawley.

"I am shocked," Miss Locke said. "Why ever would you think such a thing, Elizabeth?"

"Dr. Ryan said that my attention was too narrow. That I was concentrating too intently on Eamon Robson, rather than examining the big picture." Elizabeth lifted her cup to request a refill. "Thank you. Mrs. Sykes, you often accused me of the same thing; that I couldn't always see the forest for the trees. Well, you were right."

"I see," Mrs. Sykes prompted. "So what trees did you choose to eliminate?"

"Actually, it was Mrs. Ryan who got me started sorting out," Elizabeth allowed, "by reminding me that no one has ever successfully maneuvered the comings and goings of sharks."

Claire heaved a sigh of annoyance. "Who would want to, Elizabeth? Does your father know where you are?"

"Now, don't distract me, Claire," Elizabeth warned softly. "I messed up some by paying attention to too many unnecessary details, already."

"Go on," Mrs. Sykes urged.

"I wasn't looking at motivation. No one has been hurt so far, except for tourists. None of us in Dovekey really likes tourist season, however important it may be to us financially, so that didn't help me in pinpointing the culprit, except to assume that it is a local who is to blame."

"Very good," Mrs. Sykes praised her. "You always were a clever girl."

Sandy stood on the lawn with Dick Dawley and a much-embarrassed Pebble Beach police officer.

Dawley's feet were bare, and there was a heavy dew on the manicured grass working its way through the man's toes. The Pebble Beach mayor shifted his weight from one side to the other. A fog had rolled in off the ocean, and his short robe was feeble protection from the chill. A search warrant hung from one freckled hand.

He would have been shivering regardless of the weather.

Ginny popped the trunk of Dawley's black Camaro, and played the flashlight over the carpeted interior.

"Dick, Dick, Dick," Philbrick droned, "you are in one deep pile of it, this time."

Elizabeth continued.

"So I was going into the puzzle from the wrong end." MacKay decided not to comment. "The offenses included anaphylactic shock, an engine fire, one out-of-place snake, an equally out-of-place shark, seizure and coma of undetermined causation, and dangerous-looking trash strewn on a tourist beach.

"Very eclectic. That's what threw me, and why I blamed Dick Dawley at first. I didn't have him around all the time, so I thought he was the only one with the time and inclination. So I crossed out the things on my list that might be extraneous—which was everything except the purposeful planting of the snake and the medical trash."

"Excuse me," MacKay interrupted, "but by any chance do you have anything stronger than tea around here?"

"Why, yes," Miss Locke answered. She tottered to the pantry and pulled out a bottle of Old Overholt rye. "It was Father's," she explained and poured a shot into his tea before sitting again. "Go on, Elizabeth."

"Oh, this is stupid," Claire Wallis protested. "Elizabeth Will, you should be ashamed of yourself. You know perfectly well that none of us is a murderer. I did everything in my power to stop Eamon from having lobster that night at dinner."

Rose and Amelia simply raised their eyes to their friend, then looked away.

"That's right," Elizabeth said, remembering how unappetizing Claire had made the proposition of choosing a live lobster for execution. "You did. And you are at the hospital almost every day, too." The idea of Claire Wallis being solely responsible felt very comfy to Elizabeth, but unfortunately wrong.

MacKay came as close as he could to the act of praying that Elizabeth would wind down like a cheap watch, and soon.

"Are you through, now?" Claire asked.

"No, thank you, Claire," Elizabeth answered. "I had actually excluded the lobster dinner from the clues because Dad didn't get sick. Well, he wouldn't, would he? Because we all eat so much seafood around here in the summers, all of us have a healthy accumulated resistance to red tide. A couple of spinnerettes wouldn't fell a man of Dad's size. Wouldn't even give him gas."

"Elizabeth!" Miss Locke chastised.

"Sorry," she apologized. "Actually, MacKay tipped me off. He said everything that happened was too much for a little old lady. After watching you all work, I knew it sure wasn't too much for *three* ladies."

"Oh, for heaven's sake!" Mrs. Sykes protested. She poured a shot into her own tea, sipped, and intervened. "It was all harmless enough. All right, not exactly harmless. We all, together, decided it was time to apply the brakes to tourist season in Dovekey. Enough had become enough."

MacKay finished his tea and reached for the Old Overholt. "If no one minds." He poured.

"Not at all," Rose assented. "As a science teacher, I was best qualified to judge dosages. I can assure you, no one got a lethal dose of anything."

Elizabeth jumped in. "What do you mean by 'anything'?"

"Yes," Mrs. Sykes overlooked Elizabeth's enthusiasm, "Claire polluted the lobster tank at Lobster Haven the evening you had dinner there. You know as well as I do that no local person would ever order anything at fair market price, and certainly not lobster when we can buy it at the Market Basket for three dollars a pound.

"And you admitted yourself that Claire did everything short of expectorating into the tank to prevent Eamon from ordering from it. Nonetheless, I can assure you, the dose was too insignificant to cause convulsions."

Miss Locke put her teacup in the sink, and pulled herself as tall as she could manage.

"And I have been doctoring my rose-hip jelly with a little hemlock for, why, it must be two summers now," she admitted freely.

"That's why the tourists get a smaller jar than the locals!" Elizabeth nodded with perverse satisfaction. "To keep the adulterated separate from the regular!"

Mrs. Sykes nodded the way she did when Elizabeth was in the seventh grade.

"Very good, Elizabeth. You see, the tourists were supposed to get uncomfortable—that's all. All that was supposed to happen was that the visitors would start associating Dovekey Beach with an upset stomach. A subliminal suggestion to stay away, if you will."

"More than that, Mrs. Sykes," MacKay protested. Against his will, he was fully awake.

"Dr. MacKay"—Rose Sykes defended herself and her sister—"a full-grown adult would have to eat an entire jar to be compromised at all, and we were scrupulous about keeping it out of the hands of children. I'm sorry about Petunia, Elizabeth, but you really should enroll her in obedience school."

Elizabeth agreed, "That's true. But what about Eamon?"

It was Miss Locke's turn to be shocked.

"We were positively fastidious about that, Elizabeth. Eamon was never served the bad jelly. Really, what you must think of us to even suggest such a thing."

Elizabeth apologized immediately. She was sure Miss Locke was telling her the truth. "But, what about the fire on the *Pride of Dovekey?*"

"Oh, for heaven's sake, I did that, too," Mrs. Sykes confessed readily. "Nothing more than some oil spilled over the pistons in the engine room. There was no danger of ignition. The captain overreacted. Oh, and the shark was a red herring, too," she could not help but smile at her pun. "I just planted the idea in the child's mind and agreed with him when his overactive imagination got the best of him.

"Now, the rattlesnake was a misjudgment. Same undisciplined boy. In any event, northeastern rattlers are not very poisonous. We had nothing to do with those two old men who died, and I am still upset over that young woman. If she knew she was hypersensitive to lobster, it was moronic of her to eat shrimp. So you just go ahead and blame us for what we did, but I expect an apology from you, Elizabeth Will, for your unfounded accusations."

"Oh, boy!" was all MacKay could utter, and he did so, several times.

"Then what about Eamon?" Elizabeth worried.

MacKay snapped.

"That's really the issue for you, isn't it, Will? This is all about

Eamon Robson, and everything else be damned. You may have forgotten, but your old *friend* Martha isn't exactly in the best shape right now, either."

To her shame, Elizabeth had forgotten. And if she ever forgave MacKay for his insight, she promised herself to admit it to him.

Ginny booked Dick Dawley herself, and in the same swoop, released him on his own recognizance. But only because, if she locked him up, she would have to spend the rest of the night in her office where the lockup was located.

She was enough in touch with her emotions to realize that being alone with Dawley might be a dangerous situation—for him, at least.

To her disappointment, she only had him dead-to-rights on malicious mischief and public endangerment. She locked the heavy-gauge plastic bag containing the crushed beer-bottle fragments into the safe in her office. Sandy signed a statement witnessing the impounding of the sack.

The two women congratulated themselves on a job well done and went home to get a good night's sleep.

Frank Will was waiting up for his daughter.

Had he been the sympathetic type, which he was not, he would have commiserated with Charles MacKay instead of simply pointing the way to Avis's old room. MacKay dragged himself up the stairs unaccompanied. It had been a harrowing encounter with the Ladies' Guild of Dovekey Beach, and, as far as he could determine, establishing nothing more than an overblown plot to give innocent inlanders a case of Montezuma's revenge.

Elizabeth collapsed into a kitchen chair and allowed her father to serve her a beer and a slice of cold pepperoni pizza on a paper plate. The room seemed empty without Petunia snuffling around the floor for droppings.

"Do you know what time it is, young lady?" Frank asked.

"Spare me," Elizabeth muttered. "Tonight I have been chastised by the best. Anything you have to offer would only be second-rate."

"I heard, but I think you underestimate me, the'ah."

Elizabeth pulled on her beer thoughtfully. "I miss Mom," she said finally, surprising herself.

"Me, too," said Frank. "I would have let *her* wait up for you. Anyway, she'll be back eventually. Like they say, there's no there, there."

" 'Why should I travel?' the New Englander asked," Elizabeth quoted. "I'm already he'ah."

Frank smiled. "Ayuh. Life gets complicated when you're away from he'ah."

"Doesn't it just? I'd sure like to ask Mom a question or two about all the things I don't know about the Ladies' Guild, and the Drakes, and everything else I seem to have missed when my back was turned."

"Try me," Frank offered.

"We don't talk, Father. We banter."

"Try me," he repeated.

Elizabeth pulled a face and squirmed. "It feels unnatural."

"So, you talk; I'll listen. T'ain't much, but the folks you really need to talk to are both safe and sound in the hospital, so you're stuck with me."

With a start, Elizabeth realized that her father was dead on the money, and that she was emphatically in the wrong place at the wrong time.

"My God, that's it," she said.

"Knew I could help," Frank responded calmly.

Elizabeth ran to the kitchen door and grabbed the truck keys from the hanger next to the frame.

"Call Ginny and have her meet me at the hospital. ASAP."

Frank called out the door after Elizabeth, "You drive careful, now, I just body-puttied the back fender!"

Charles MacKay roused briefly at the noise, rolled over, and fell back into a stuporous sleep.

Frank dialed the rotary wall phone, cursed, hung up, and dialed again.

Elizabeth accelerated the old truck until it started the shimmy that announced that it had been pushed as far as it was willing to go, without spitting engine parts all over the beach road. The sun was just uncurling over the lip of the ocean to her right, and the road was deserted.

She aborted her plan to switch over to the highway, and stuck to the more-circuitous, but less-traveled route. The tires squealed in protest as she tore around corners faster than she ought. No worries about a speeding ticket; the entire Dovekey Beach police department was either asleep or following behind.

Rather than waste even a second for the automatic door, Elizabeth battered her way through the manual emergency entrance of the regional hospital and raced past the deserted triage nurse's station without a second glance. Her sandals slid on the highly polished tiles as she made a turn to the one-bed ICU, and she careered off the pastel pink cinder block wall.

Through the intensive-care door window, she could see the night-duty nurse slumped in the vinyl armchair beside Eamon's bed, but Eamon Robson's face was hidden behind the dark figure that stood, obstructing her view. The life-monitoring systems were shut down and silent.

Elizabeth pushed on the brass plate slowly but deliberately, so as not to startle Eamon's early morning visitor.

"Martha?" Elizabeth spoke softly. "Martha, it's me. It's Biz, Martha."

"He can't eat," Martha told her friend. The sleeping nurse opened her eyes and leaned forward, dropping her book to the floor.

"It's all right," Elizabeth hurriedly explained. Taking her cue, the nurse carefully swept up the novel and stood. "Why don't you get a cup of coffee while Martha and I watch over Eamon?" The nurse nodded without saying a word and slipped past the two women and out the door.

"I brought it special," Martha said, lifting the jar slightly. "It's Eamon's favorite, but he won't swallow. See?" she indicated Eamon's lips, smeared pink with rose-hip jelly. "So I'm waiting."

"I'll wait with you, Martha. And Ginny's on her way, too. It'll be just like the old days; the three of us."

Martha tilted her head, seeming to mull over the proposition. Then, she snorted amusement.

"Just exactly."

Elizabeth tried to move Martha from her vigilant position over Eamon's bed and into the chair near the window, but Martha was rooted. Elizabeth comforted herself by rubbing small circles on Martha's back.

"Martha," she asked in a low voice, "are you going to have a baby?" There was no response. The tall, cool blonde's eyes never wavered from her husband's lips. "Marty?"

"Is it time?" Martha asked.

"Time for what?" Elizabeth sneaked a look at the door, wanting very much to see the face of someone with some psychiatric training. She knew it would be another five minutes before Ginny could possibly get herself awake, dressed, and to the hospital.

"To have the baby," Martha answered. "That's why I'm here in the hospital, isn't it?"

"I don't know, Martha. Is that why you came home?"

"Uh-huh," she nodded. "They take babies away in Canada, so I had to come home. I'm married this time. I had to keep Eamon here."

"How, Marty? What did you do?"

"When I saw Miss Locke making her jelly with the other berries, I just made sure that Eamon got enough to make him stay, you understand."

With enormous relief, Elizabeth heard the door open behind her. She continued to rub her friend's back. "Oh, Marty."

"Martha Ann Drake!" Frank spoke loudly in the small room. "There you are." Martha turned to Elizabeth's father like a sunflower turning to the light.

"Mr. Will," she said.

"Your parents have been looking high and low for you, young lady. Now"—he took her arm and walked her over to the chair and settled her into it—"you sit right here so we don't lose you again."

"I didn't do anything," Martha protested.

"I know that, Marty. T'wasn't your fault, and that's what I'm gonna tell your folks. We're gonna talk all of this right out into the daylight, and everything's gonna be right as rain. Isn't that right, Lizzie?"

Elizabeth broke from her frozen position and went to her friend. "That's right," she agreed. "You won't be punished, Marty, I promise."

"Cross your heart and hope to die?"

"Stick a needle in my eye," Elizabeth swore and pulled Martha's head to her shoulder. She rocked slowly as Frank looked on.

"Ginny's on her way," Frank whispered. "She had the by-gawd phone off the hook, so I had to stop by the carriage house and wake her up."

"How did you get here?" Elizabeth asked.

"Always wanted to get behind the wheel of that biostitute bastard's ninety-thousand-dollar van."

"You stole MacKay's van?"

"Semantics," Frank answered as Ginny flung open the door.

EPILOGUE

"We were keeping it a secret," Eamon said. Elizabeth shook her head sadly. He got up from the Wills' kitchen table and stretched. MacKay spread his cards faceup on the table and pulled the poker chips toward him. "She said she wanted to wait until the second trimester before she told you all that she was pregnant. Martha has always been conservative like that." Eamon laughed bitterly at himself. "What am I saying? I guess I don't have a clue what Martha has always been like. Maybe even *she* doesn't know." Avis handed him a cup of coffee and went back to doing the dishes. Sandy dried. "I guess her nesting instinct got the best of her, and I didn't pay attention."

"It's the way she was raised," Elizabeth absolved him. "She had no idea that Claire had polluted your lobster and Claire thought you were free of the jelly. You were accidentally double-whammied."

MacKay dealt again. "We're all part of a secret society around here."

"Speaking of secrets," Ginny anteed up and threw down two cards. "I got ahold of Martha's parents courtesy of the British

Columbia RCMP. There's something to be said for a Big Brother society: Those federal health cards are more permanent than tattoos."

"Are they coming?" Eamon asked. Frank looked at the young man with weary empathy, but did not say anything.

"No," Ginny answered. She picked up her two new cards and studied them for a moment. Elizabeth kicked her under the table. "Eamon, did you know that the Drakes are raising Martha's daughter as their own?"

Eamon leaned against the counter, and reached down to stroke Petunia's ears. "I guess I suspected. The way they just packed up and left as soon as we married. My stubborn chauvinism was the final straw, I guess. There was always something frighteningly cold about the way Martha's family acted toward one another."

"Can't take that to mean anything, boy," Frank raised MacKay's bet and lifted an eyebrow to psych the other man out. "Elizabeth claims to be an orphan all the time. I don't take it personally. If I did, I'd probably move to Canada myself."

Elizabeth folded her hand with a slap. "Eamon, weren't you applying for alien residency and planning to get your citizenship?"

"What? No. That was the problem. What would make you think that?"

Avis cleared her throat accusingly and continued with the dishes. Elizabeth rose above her sister's condemnation.

"I saw some applications, and assumed."

Steely-eyed, Frank doubled his bet. "When one assumes, one makes an ass—"

"Call," MacKay cut him off, platituded out of his mind.

Eamon took his coffee to the table. "That was Martha's dream. I could never understand why it was so important to her. Elizabeth, we had a good life in Canada. What a mess!"

Ginny threw three chips into the pot. "See you." The men

had been bluffing each other and threw their hands into the middle of the table. "What are you going to do, Eamon? Martha will be in Concord for psychiatric evaluation for a while. The State is obligated to bring charges against her for attempted murder."

Eamon Robson rubbed his eyes and pushed himself away from the game. "I'm going to give my wife a present. I dropped my alien resident forms at Immigration in Newington this morning." MacKay could not help but notice the look of absolute adoration Elizabeth cast on the immigrant flanker. "We all know she was not competent. She had no idea that Claire was spiking my food, too. I really believe she would have stopped if she'd known."

No one else in the room was so confident, but, of course, they did not see fit to disagree. After all, it was none of their business.

Eamon continued, "When she's released, I'm taking Martha to upstate New York at least until the baby is born. It's really important to her that the baby is American. IBM has offered me a position."

"We'll miss you," Elizabeth said sadly. "But it will be good to know we've started a new generation of DARs. Will you let us know where you end up?"

"Eventually," Eamon answered. "For a while I think it would be better if Martha got some distance. I'm driving to Concord tomorrow; the doctors said it would be all right."

Everyone nodded. It would have been rude to inquire further.

"Well," Ginny stacked her chips and cashed herself out, "I have a big day tomorrow. They're letting the Ladies' Guild of Dovekey Beach out of Brentwood Psychiatric first thing. I expect Claire is going to be a Tasmanian devil of indignation."

" 'Spect you're right," Frank agreed, following suit. "Fact

is, no one died from their meddling. Don't know what the penalty is for criminal misdemeanor."

"I'm recommending life for Dick Dawley," Ginny said.

When all but the Wills and Charles MacKay remained in the drafty old Cape Cod, Elizabeth tried to organize a group viewing of the silent version of *Nosferatu,* running on Channel 56, and was soundly rejected.

Sullenly, she walked MacKay to his van.

"Hey," he said at the car, "what are you doing Saturday?"

Elizabeth was taken aback. Hard to believe it took so little after the events of the previous week, but she was.

"Saturday?" She pretended to think about it. "Rugby?"

"We're playing the Boston Irish. Lots of blood guaranteed."

"You did say Saturday." Elizabeth leaned against the van.

"Date night." MacKay kissed her. "Saturday. We're going to get killed. A woman with your propensities ought to love it."

Elizabeth kissed MacKay back.

"It's a date."

WITHDRAWN